TWEEN FICTION M

SOMETHING
WICKED'S
IN THOSE WOODS

Marisa Montes

HARCOURT, INC.

San Diego   New York   London

Library of Congress Cataloging-in-Publication Data
Montes, Marisa.
Something wicked's in those woods/Marisa Montes.—1st ed.
p.   cm.
Summary: When their parents are killed in an accident, eleven-year-old Javier
and his younger brother leave their home in Puerto Rico to go live with their
aunt in northern California, where a ghost from an unsolved crime and Javi's
newfound psychokinetic powers make their adjustment all the harder.
[1. Supernatural—Fiction.   2. Parapsychology—Fiction.   3. Ghosts—Fiction.
4. Brothers—Fiction.   5. Puerto Ricans—United States—Fiction.
6. California, Northern—Fiction.]   I. Title.
PZ7.M76365So   2000
[Fic]—dc21   99-58755
ISBN 0-15-202391-7

Text set in Janson MT
Designed by Lori McThomas Buley

First edition
A C E G H F D B

Printed in the United States of America

Acknowledgments:
*Special thanks to my aunt, Dr. Carmín Montes Cumming, for being my Spanish-
language consultant and for always encouraging me to write. Thanks also to
my critique-group members Corinne Hawkins and Debbie Novak, for their
suggestions, encouragement, and support during a very difficult time in my life;
to my mentor, Barbara A. Steiner, for teaching me to "tighten, tighten, tighten";
and especially to Elizabeth Koehler-Pentacoff, for bringing in a fresh point of view
and for helping me to plug up those last pesky holes. Thank you most of all
to Karen Grove, my editor, for helping my dreams come true.*

To my husband, David Plotkin,
for his constant loyalty and for carrying
me through those difficult times.
And to my parents, Rubén and Mary Montes,
who taught me to be proud of my family
and to love the island of my birth.

SOMETHING WICKED'S IN THOSE WOODS

FOG CLUNG SO TIGHTLY to the black Volvo that Javi was
surprised the car could still run smoothly up the winding
highway. He'd never seen anything like it. Thick and gray,
like smoke—no, like a rain cloud that had fallen to earth.
Clumps of fog slid along the windows, giving way almost
reluctantly, as though they had been struggling to seep in
through the edges of the glass but were ripped away at the
last moment by the speed of the car. Watching them reminded him of how he had wanted to creep out the air-
plane window before it took off, before it snatched him
from the only home he'd ever known, bringing him to this.

Javi couldn't decide which was worse, being able to see
only a few feet ahead or watching cars whip by on the
biggest highway he'd ever seen—four lanes coming and
four lanes going! He knew the highway was out there only
because the fog had been lighter when they left the San

Francisco airport with their aunt. It had begun to thicken the moment they got off the Bay Bridge, following signs to Oakland, then to Highway 24.

A cold, clammy hand snuck into Javi's and squeezed. He turned to his little brother. Nico's eyes were dark moons against his small, pale face. He clutched Pulito, his floppy stuffed dog, about the neck in a stranglehold that would have made a live dog's eyes pop. Javi scooched toward Nico and pulled him close. His gaze slid back to the side window.

As they continued uphill, their aunt's car slowed. An enormous black archway loomed ahead, gaping. The Volvo lurched forward, breaking through the gray swirls and into a long, dark tunnel. Wisps of fog escorted them inside, then released them to the fluorescent lights that whizzed by overhead.

Nico leaned into Javi and buried his face in Pulito's fur. Javi knew Nico had never been inside a tunnel. Neither had he, really. He'd seen them on television and in the movies, and San Juan had a few short tunnels, but nothing like this. It seemed to go on forever, winding downward through the throat of the mountain as though they were descending into the belly of a dragon.

As Javi stared, mesmerized, the tunnel fell away and the world became brilliant sunlight and sea blue sky. Tree-covered hills rushed along either side of the highway, and explosions of pink and red and white oleander filled the center divide. He blinked against the sun and nudged Nico.

Nico nestled further into his side.

"*Mira,* Nico, look," Javi whispered in Spanish. "It's okay. Look." He pushed Nico away and pulled Pulito from his face.

Nico opened one eye, then the other. His eyes

widened. "Are we in Oz?" Those were the first words he'd spoken since their parents' accident.

Javi smiled, despite his resolution never again to be agreeable. "I don't think so."

"What was that?" Amparo Leál turned slightly, keeping one eye on the road.

"*Nada,* Tití Amparo, nothing," Javi replied. "Nico was just wondering if we were there yet."

"Almost. Another five minutes is all," their aunt replied in Spanish. Switching to English, she added, "Javier, I'd like you to speak only English for a while—until you're as comfortable with it as you are with Spanish."

Javi groaned. "But, Tití, at home, also?"

"Yes, at home. You've got to become as fluent as the other kids in your new school. You don't want to fall behind, do you?"

"Nico, also? I no can speak English to Nico. He only a baby—he no yet learn the English."

"He'll learn faster than you think. But all right. For now, you may continue to speak Spanish to Nicolás—but he's the only one."

Despite the bright sunshine, Javi felt as though he were on the other side of the tunnel, smothering in fog. He glared at the image of his aunt's face in the rearview mirror. She looked up, and their eyes met. Javi looked away.

Amparo sighed. "Javier, I know how rough this past month has been, and I'm not trying to make things tougher—quite the opposite. If you were only five, like Nicolás, and going into kindergarten, that would be different. You'd be fluent in English by the time you had to learn to read and write. But you're going into sixth grade in an English-speaking school—"

"I go to an English-speaking school in Puerto Rico,

and Mami and Papi no make me speak the English at home."

"That's because most of the other kids were Puerto Rican, too. And you were all learning English at about the same rate. If you didn't understand something, the teacher could explain it in Spanish. No one is going to speak Spanish to you in this school, except in Spanish class. And I don't want them to. You need to learn English so well you can think in English. Then we'll start speaking Spanish at home again—so you won't forget."

Amparo veered the car off the highway and onto a road that led them uphill into a dense forest of ancient gnarled oaks. Like giant, multilimbed ghouls, the trees reached out to the passing car, beckoning, hovering, waiting. At their feet, ferns and brambles and underbrush grew thick and wild.

The road narrowed and wound farther uphill and into the woods, leaving behind the brilliant sunshine and clear blue sky, taking on Javi's somber mood.

Nico tugged Javi's sleeve. "Is this the Forest of No Return?" he whispered in his big brother's ear.

"I'm afraid so," Javi whispered back.

"HERE WE ARE," Amparo said.

The car pulled off the winding road and onto a long gravel driveway, bumpy with potholes and tree roots and shrouded by a canopy of interlocking branches. Amparo stopped before a two-story, natural-wood house in a small clearing surrounded by tall pines and heavy oaks.

The windows were dark and unwelcoming. Javi shifted uneasily in his seat. A large door rolled up before them, exposing a black hole of a room. Nico's cold hand slid into Javi's again. The car crept into the room and stopped. Then the door rolled back down, enveloping them in darkness.

"The lightbulb burned out in the garage-door opener," said Amparo, getting out of the car. "Stay there till I turn on the main light."

Javi was in no hurry to go into the gloomy wooden house. He didn't know what he'd expected, but certainly not this! In Puerto Rico, the houses were made of sturdy concrete and were painted either solid white or pastel colors. And there were neighborhoods, with houses next to houses, welcoming houses, warm houses, with lawns and flowers and palm trees. Like his house. Mami and Papi's house ...

"Javier? Nicolás?" their aunt called. "Come on out now. The light is on. Be careful climbing these stairs—there's no rail—"

"We're not clumsy. We know how to climb stairs."

"English, please, Javier."

Javi glared at his aunt. But he took Nico's hand and helped him up the stairs, just in case.

"Watch out for the pets. I don't want you tripping over them and hurting yourselves." Amparo unlocked the door and pushed the boys inside, shutting the kitchen door behind her.

The kitchen filled with the sounds of yelping and of scraping claws on wooden floors. Sliding around the counter came a wriggling black blur. In the next instant, a small black Scottie was jumping, wriggling, yelping, panting, and drooling all over Amparo, then Javi, then Nico, then Amparo again.

"Okay, boy, calm down." Amparo knelt and scratched the squirming mass of fur. "*Muchachos,* meet Fidel Castro. Fidel, say hi to the boys."

"Fidel Castro?" Javi said before he could stop himself.

Amparo held up the dog's face for the boys to examine. "Look at this black beard and tell me he doesn't look like Castro."

Nico knelt and touched Fidel's nose. The little dog licked the boy's fingers and squirmed free of his mistress's grasp. Pouncing on Nico, Fidel toppled him onto the floor and licked his face. Nico squealed with musical giggles.

To Javi, the sound of his brother's laughter could be topped only by the sound of his parents' voices. For the second time that day, he smiled. Then something pushed hard against his legs, making him stumble forward.

"Ah, ZsaZsa." Amparo scooped up a fluffy white Persian and held the cat against her face. "You don't like not being the center of attention, do you, princess? Would you like to hold her, Javier?" Amparo placed the cat in Javi's arms. "Javier Arturo Leál Cisneros, meet ZsaZsa Gatór. Get it? Like the actress Zsa Zsa Gabor?"

Javi made no comment about his aunt's clever wordplay, making *gato,* the Spanish word for "cat," rhyme with "Gabor." As he held the cat gingerly, ZsaZsa nuzzled her face against his chin. "*Me besa*—I mean, she kiss me."

Amparo shook her head. "She's marking you. With her scent."

"*Ooiii!*" Javi dumped the cat on the floor. He wiped his chin with the back of his hand. "That's . . . *desagradable.*"

Amparo smiled. " 'Disgusting' in English. But here in the States, a child your age would probably say 'gross.' "

"Are there more"—Javi flicked his hand distastefully toward ZsaZsa—"animals gross?"

At first Amparo looked puzzled, then she smiled. "You mean 'gross animals,' not 'animals gross.' In English, the adjective precedes the noun." Amparo shrugged off her jacket and hung it on a coatrack. "Actually, there is one more pet. But she's definitely not gross."

Javi grimaced, deciding it was probably *more* gross. While his aunt stepped out to get their suitcases and Nico played with Fidel, Javi looked around.

The kitchen was dark, as he had suspected it would be, and the fluorescent lighting did little to brighten it. The ever-present trees outside kept the house in constant shadow. And the dark walnut cabinets that lined two of the four walls, as well as the dark oak floors, added to the heavy gloom. Even the counter tiling was a dark blue.

But the stone fireplace in the adjoining family room might add some cheeriness to the place when lit up, Javi thought. He'd never been in a house with a fireplace. It might be nice.

Something else he found interesting was what looked like an indoor barbecue—right there in the kitchen! An arch set into a chimney next to the stove formed the barbecue pit. A rotisserie bar ran across the middle of the arch, and a grill covered the bottom.

"Tití," he said when Amparo came back, "is this *una barbacoa?*"

"A barbecue? Yes, in fact, I bought us steaks for tonight—to celebrate your first night in your new home."

"May we ... may we roast a pig someday?"

"A pig?" Amparo threw back her head and laughed. "Me? Cook a pig?" When her eyes met Javi's, she stopped laughing. "*Ahem,* well ... a pig. Why don't we start with a duck or a small chicken first? Then we'll see."

Javi nodded, pretending he really didn't care.

"Javier, why don't you and Nicolás take Fidel to the backyard for his walk? In the meantime I'll make lunch. You kids must be starved."

Amparo clipped a leash to Fidel's collar and handed it to Javi. She led them through a long hallway, past a wooden staircase, and into a cozy office. A desk piled with stacks of papers was tucked in the far corner next to a stone fireplace. (*Two fireplaces in one house!* thought Javi.) Bookcases stuffed with books covered two of the walls, and another wall, made of plate glass, overlooked a small clearing edged by dense woods. In the middle of the scene, beneath a natural archway of interlocking branches, a wooden footbridge crossed a tiny stream.

A sliding glass door opened onto a wooden deck.

"Don't go far," Amparo said, sliding the door open. "Lunch should be ready soon."

Fidel yelped and tugged frantically at the leash, pulling Javi down the stairs. "Wait, wait, you pesky *perrito*. My arm!"

Nico giggled and plunked down on the top step to watch. Javi walked around the yard, waiting by every bush and tree trunk while Fidel sniffed and inspected, choosing the best spot at which to lift his leg.

The woods seemed unusually silent. *Were birds chirping and insects buzzing when we first came out?* Javi thought. As he stood by a bush, waiting for Fidel to finish his business, Javi got a strange, prickling sensation at the back of his neck. Odd . . . was someone—?

Javi thought he caught a movement from the corner of his eye. He snapped his head around. Leaves fluttered in an old oak near the footbridge, as though a breeze had just passed, but nothing was there. He was about to turn back around when Fidel's low growl made his muscles tense.

The little dog was glaring at the old oak. His lips curled back in an ugly snarl. He growled from deep in his throat, sounding like a much larger dog. Suddenly Fidel lurched forward, barking and snarling, yanking Javi's arm and almost ripping free.

Javi held tight and pulled him back. "What is wrong, *perrito*? What do you see?"

A voice behind Javi answered, "Something wicked's in those woods."

JAVI SPUN AROUND.

He was met with nothing but the thick trunk of another oak. He glanced at the house. Nico was still perched on the top step. His head was cocked to one side, and he was absorbed with something at the bottom of the steps.

"You hear someone, Fidel?" Javi whispered.

Fidel had lost interest in whatever he had spotted in the woods and was sniffing around the foot of the oak.

"I said, something wicked's in those woods," the voice repeated.

With a happy bark, Fidel rose on his hind legs and scratched the tree trunk with his forepaws. His stubby tail wagged in greeting, and his jaws parted in a doggie grin.

Javi studied the thick branches of the oak. At first he saw nothing. Then a slight rustling caused him to step closer and peer upward.

A small figure peeled away from a branch and slid to a lower limb, emerging from the foliage as though it were part of it. Hiking boots and camouflage pants dangled before Javi's eyes. A long, shimmering curtain of chestnut hair came next, swinging from the upside-down scalp of a tanfaced girl.

The girl extended a hand. "Hi, I'm Willo. You must be Javier."

"I . . . yes, I am Javier—Javi." He examined the extended arm, wondering how to shake an upside-down hand, and finally decided to grasp the fingertips.

"Well, Javier-Javi, I thought you'd never get here."

"I am Javier or Javi, no 'Javier-Javi.' Who are you? How you know me?"

"Crickets! I told you—I'm Willo." As if that explained everything, the girl pulled herself right side up and gazed down, studying him as though he were a curious new species of wildlife.

"Willow?" Javi had to admit, the girl did remind him of a tree. "How you know my name?"

"You speak English quite well. I don't see what Amparo was worried about."

"You no answer questions quite well."

Willo snorted and jumped from the branch, landing before him with the grace of a cat. "Okay, what would you like to know?"

"You no listen quite well, either." Now it was Javi's turn to study the annoying girl.

Right side up, her straight hair hung far below her waist, glistening as it cascaded over the curves of her head and shoulders like water over rocks. She was Javi's height and, beneath her baggy camouflage pants and khaki tank top, very slim. Her skin was as tan as tamarind pods, and her hazel eyes appeared to change with her surroundings, like chameleons. Up in the tree they looked oak-leaf green; next to the tree trunk they turned ash gray. And their stare seemed to hold him in a trance, deep and intense, so that Javi finally had to look away.

When he looked back, she was grinning. A cocky, annoying grin that told him she knew she'd won the staring contest. It also seemed to say that winning wasn't a new experience for her.

"Actually, I do listen quite well. I simply like to choose which questions to answer." She crossed her arms and leaned against the tree. "Let me see . . . you wanted to know how I know your name. Daddy and I are friends of Amparo. She and Daddy teach at the university in Berkeley—Daddy teaches English literature and Amparo teaches psychology. Anyway, she told us you and Nicolás were coming from Puerto Rico to live with her since . . . I'm sorry about your parents."

Javi winced. He still wasn't used to talking about his parents' death. And he didn't want anyone's pity—especially a strange girl's.

She continued, "I know how it is—"

Javi scowled at the girl. "You cannot know! How can you?"

"I do know—my mother died four years ago!" Willo glared back, staring him down again. But this time her gaze softened under Javi's defiant glare, and she lowered her voice. "Losing one parent isn't quite the same as losing both, and at the same time . . . But no matter how wonderful Daddy is, he can't take Mom's place. I'll never stop missing her."

Javi swallowed and stooped to pet Fidel, burying his hot tears in warm fur.

"So, anyway," Willo went on, squatting beside Javi, "Amparo was concerned that you'd have a tough time in school because you don't speak much English—"

"I speak enough," Javi mumbled to Fidel.

"That's what I just said. But I suppose she didn't know . . ."

"So she ask you to . . . what is it called—baby-sit?"

"No, really—"

"I am not a baby to sit with." Javi eyed Willo once more. "I have eleven years. How many years you have?"

"Years? Oh! You mean you're eleven years old?"

Javi nodded. "Eleven years old . . . yes."

"Well, I'm eleven, too. That's why I volunteered to help you out—show you around town, introduce you to some kids, help you with your English and all."

Javi stared at the girl in stony silence.

"See, Amparo and I are friends. And since you and I are both going into the sixth grade, I thought we could be—"

"Why have you the name of a tree?" Javi said, not yet wanting to consider the possibility of friendship.

"A tree? Crocs on a rock!" Willo snorted again. "My name isn't Willow with a *w* at the end. It's just Willo." She spelled it for him.

Javi nodded, visualizing. "No *w* at the end." He gave some thought to his next sentence. "Up in the tree, you see something bad in the woods?"

" 'You *saw* something bad,' past tense." She corrected him with the air of a practiced teacher. "No, I didn't see anything, but I could feel it. I've felt it before, but it was especially strong today—when you were near the footbridge with Fidel."

"You play too much in the woods?"

"I love the woods, especially near my house. I've spent

most of my life hiking in the woods. But around here, I don't know ... there's something sinister about these woods."

"Sinister?"

"It means 'ominous, wicked, evil.'"

"Ominous," Javi said, testing the syllables, listening to their sounds. He glanced at the spot where he thought he'd seen movement. He shivered, remembering the prickling sensation on the back of his neck. "Wicked ... evil ..."

"Javier! Nicolás! Lunch is ready." Amparo popped her head out the door. "Javier— Willo, how nice to see you! Would you stay for lunch? I made plenty."

"Sure, love to," Willo replied.

"Javier, where's Nicolás?"

"He—" Javi looked at the top step, where Nico had been sitting only a few minutes before. "He sit there."

"Don't worry," said Willo, "the only way out of the yard is the footbridge. I would have noticed if he'd crossed it."

"Here, let me take Fidel." Amparo took the leash. "You kids search outside. I'll search the house."

Javi and Willo searched the back and side yards up to the front fences. Willo crawled under the deck while Javi checked under bushes, both calling, "Nico! Nico, where are you?"

But there was no sign of Nico.

With each passing minute, Javi's stomach grew more knotted. He fought down a wave of panic. What would he do if something happened to Nico, the last member of his family?

AS TERROR TUGGED at the back of Javi's throat and tears threatened to spill from his eyes, he heard Fidel's excited bark. Then the door opened and Amparo called out, "Found him! Javier, Willo!"

Javi raced around the side of the house and up the steps. When he saw his little brother peering at him sheepishly from Amparo's side, Javi grabbed him and hugged him close. Then realizing how foolish he must look to be panicking when Nico was gone for only a few minutes, Javi released him and stood up.

"Where was he?" he asked his aunt.

"Playing hide-and-seek." Amparo sounded both relieved and annoyed.

"Who was he playing hide-and-seek with?" Willo slipped past Javi and plunked down on a leather couch in the corner of the den.

"Apparently he made a new friend and wouldn't come out until the friend found him."

"A friend?" Javi looked puzzled.

Amparo sighed. "As far as I can make out, he got bored and came inside, then discovered Misifú."

"Misifú?"

Amparo nodded and pointed behind him. A fat, long-haired tabby with white feet sauntered into the den. The moment she saw them, she plopped down, blinked as though nothing could be more boring than humans, and proceeded to wash her face.

Nico flew to the tabby's side. He pulled up under her front legs, stretching the cat until she was almost as tall as he was. He tried to pick her up, but she was so heavy he had to half drag, half carry her to the couch.

"*Ah*, the third animal gross." Javi eyed the fat cat with distaste.

"The what?" asked Willo.

"I mean, gross animal." Javi's face flushed.

"Misifú's not gross, are you, girl?" Willo gave the cat a fond squeeze.

"Well"—Amparo stepped to the door—"shall we eat?"

Javi and Willo followed Amparo to the kitchen, where the table was set for three. A large bowl of potato salad sat in the middle.

"Willo," said Amparo, "you know where the plates and silverware are. Why don't you set a place for yourself while I boil up another hot dog?"

"None for me, thanks. I'll stick with the potato salad. Looks delicious."

"Sorry, Willo, I forgot you're strictly vegetarian."

"You never eat McDonald's?" Javi couldn't imagine giving up hamburgers.

Willo set her plate and silverware next to Javi's and sat down. "I can eat their french fries and hot apple pies. You have McDonald's in Puerto Rico?"

Javi nodded. "And Burger King and others. And we have *lechonerias* where they sell *lechón asado*." Javi glanced longingly at the indoor barbecue.

"What's that?" Willo helped herself to some potato salad.

Amparo rolled her eyes and sighed. "Roast pig. It appears to be one of Javier's favorite foods."

Willo shuddered. "Poor pig!"

As Amparo brought the hot dogs and buns to the table, she glanced around. "Now, where's Nicolás gone off to again?"

"Still with Misifú, probably," said Willo. "I didn't notice him following us into the kitchen."

"I find him, Tití." Javi dashed into the hall. He couldn't believe he'd lost track of his little brother twice in one hour. Since their parents' accident, they'd hardly been out of each other's sight.

As he approached the den, he heard giggles. *Nico must be playing with Fidel again,* he thought. He stopped to listen for a moment, enjoying his brother's babylike shrieks of joy. But when he entered, Javi froze in midstep.

Nico was rolling on the floor by himself. He was struggling and kicking playfully, as though wrestling with an invisible partner.

From the safety of the couch, Misifú observed the display with a distinctly bored expression. Her eyes were half closed and only her ears twitched, whenever Nico let out a particularly loud shriek.

At one point Nico pushed his hands against something above him, giggling helplessly and crying, "*¡No más, no más cosquillas!* No tickles, no tickles!"

"Nico? What are you doing?" Javi asked in Spanish.

Nico stopped thrashing and lay back, his chest heaving.

"Nico, did you hear me? I said, what are you doing?"

"Playing tickles."

"Like we used to play with Papi?"

Nico nodded.

"But you were alone. How can you play tickles alone?"

"Javi *bobo*, I'm not alone." Nico stood and pointed.

Javi glanced at Misifú and ruffled his brother's golden-brown hair. "You're the silly one. Nico *bobo*, playing tickles alone."

Nico tugged at his arm. "We're hungry."

"Yes, we are. So hurry up. Tití has lunch ready." Javi took Nico's hand and led him to the kitchen. All the way Nico kept looking back, as if he'd left something behind. "Hurry, Nico, the hot dogs will get cold. You can play with that fat old cat later."

At the table, Javi helped Nico into his chair, then sat down between Willo and Amparo.

While the others ate, Nico kept turning to look at something in the hall.

"What is it, Nico?" Javi asked, putting down his hot dog.

"Don't you like hot dogs?" Amparo spoke to Nico in Spanish.

Nico nodded and grinned.

"Then why aren't you eating?" she asked.

"I'm waiting for my new friend. I don't want him to go hungry." Nico pulled out the chair beside him. "He can sit here and share my hot dog."

Amparo leaned over and stroked Nico's cheek. "What a considerate little boy you are. But Misifú won't go hungry. Misifú has her own food that she eats at certain times. And we mustn't encourage the pets to eat at the table."

Nico looked behind him. He patted the chair next to him and signaled, beckoning. "Javi and I have new friends. We share our lunch."

"Nico, didn't you hear me? Misifú can't eat with us."

Nico nodded. "I know." He cut his hot dog and bun in half and laid them on the place mat in front of the empty chair. As Javi stared in disbelief, Nico took a big bite of his half and grinned. *"Mmm-mmm."*

"Nico," asked Javi, "what are you doing?"

"Eating," Nico mumbled.

"But why did you put half your lunch on the empty place mat? Tití just told you Misifú is not supposed to eat at the table. Put the rest of your hot dog on your own plate."

Nico shook his head and kept eating.

"Nico—"

Amparo placed her hand on Javi's shoulder. "It's all right, Javier. Nicolás is just having a little trouble adjusting. He's testing his limits . . . and mine."

"But he has never acted this way before."

"He's never been away from home before. Let's give him time."

"I don't know. Something's wrong." Something that had been nagging at the back of Javi's mind clicked. "Nico, where did you learn the word 'tickles'? You've always called it *cosquillas*. How did you learn the English word?"

Nico took a sip of milk, leaving a creamy mustache. "My new friend."

Javi gave a frustrated sigh and turned to his aunt.

"Nico," Amparo began softly, "tell us about this new friend. Where is he now?"

Nico smiled and pointed to the chair beside him.

The chair was still empty.

5

"WHAT'S GOING ON?" said Willo. "Why are you guys staring at an empty chair?"

"I'm sorry, Willo," Amparo replied. "I forgot we were speaking Spanish. Nicolás doesn't speak English yet. It appears his new friend is not Misifú. It seems that he wants a new friend like his big brother has, so he's invented one. The friend is supposedly sitting in the chair beside him."

Willo eyed the empty chair, the uneaten piece of hot dog, then Nico. "Oh, an imaginary friend. No big deal, Javi. I had one when I was little."

"*No tiene sentido.*" Javi shook his head. "No make sense. Nico never do this before."

"'*It does not* make sense'—present tense," said Willo. "'Nico never *did* this'—past tense."

Javi glared at Willo.

Amparo patted his shoulder. "Javier, if the past month

has been difficult for you, imagine how difficult it must have been for a five-year-old. This is simply his way of dealing with what has happened."

"Trust Amparo, Javi. Shrinks know about these things." At Javi's puzzled look, Willo added, "A *shrink* is a psychologist."

Javi glanced at his brother. Nico swung his legs happily as he munched his hot dog. He seemed the same as always, and yet—

"Tití, you should see him this past month. He is sad and do not talk. Now he laugh, he talk. Very strange."

"Those are good things, Javier. Maybe the healing process has begun."

Javi looked down at his plate.

"Javier? Is that it? Are you worried that Nicolás is beginning to forget your parents?"

Javi frowned. "Nico never forget! I never forget!"

"Of course you won't forget. But don't you want Nicolás to stop hurting?"

Javi pushed a chunk of potato around the plate with his fork. He didn't want his little brother to keep feeling the same pain he was feeling. Maybe Amparo was right. Maybe he was making a big thing over Nico's imaginary friend because he wished he, too, could laugh and play and be carefree again.

"Javier?"

At that moment Fidel trotted into the room and wandered over to the chair next to Nico—the one occupied by the imaginary friend. He gave a happy bark and wagged his tail, wriggling as though he were greeting an old friend.

"Fidel!" said Amparo. "You know better than to beg at the table. Sit down, sit!"

Fidel obeyed his mistress but kept glancing at the empty chair and doggie-grinning. His tail thumped the floor.

Javi spotted the place mat next to Nico. "Nico, what happened to the other half of the hot dog?"

"He must have eaten it while we were talking," said Willo.

"Did you eat it, Nico?"

Nico shook his head and sipped more milk.

"Did you give it to Fidel?" Amparo asked in an accusing tone.

Again Nico shook his head.

"Well," said Javi, "where is it?"

"Hamish ate it."

"Who?"

Nico pointed at the empty chair.

Amparo took over. "Tell us your new friend's name, Nicolás."

Nico cupped his hand at the side of his mouth and whispered to the chair. Then he leaned toward the chair, listening. His lips moved but made no sound, as if he were memorizing. He whispered again and nodded.

"His name is Hamish Brenden McTavish."

Javi's mouth gaped. He swallowed. "How—how did you make up a name like that?"

"THIS IS YOUR NEW HOME, *muchachos.*"

Amparo had sat the boys down in the family room for a talk. For Nico's sake, she had shifted to Spanish.

"I know it's not what you're used to, but I'll do my best to make us a family. I want you to feel comfortable. When you're hungry, you're welcome to anything in the kitchen—you don't have to ask. If anything is bothering you, I'm ready to listen. If you want or need anything, tell me. I may not be able to give you everything you want, but I want you to feel comfortable asking."

Amparo looked to the boys for comment. Nico was busy tying and untying his shoelaces. Javi bumped him with his elbow. Nico looked up questioningly, then smiled and nodded at his aunt. Javi said nothing.

"I'm also going to need your help," Amparo continued. "I can't learn to raise two boys, keep working, take care of three pets, and do all the housekeeping myself. I'll need you both to help around the house, especially you, Javier."

Amparo glanced at Javi. He tensed. Tiny frown lines formed between his eyebrows.

She smiled. "Don't worry, Javier, it's not anything that most children your age aren't expected to do."

Javi stood. "Mami and Papi didn't expect us to do anything around the house."

Amparo motioned for Javi to sit back down. "Javier, you know your mother quit working when you were born. It was her choice, and she enjoyed being a homemaker. But I can't do that"—Amparo looked at Nico, then Javi—"and I wouldn't want to. I love my job, and we need the income. The only way I can keep working is if you help out. Anyway, it's good for you to learn to share the responsibility."

At the word "responsibility," Javi clenched his jaw. In the past month, he had felt as though he'd had to take on a lifetime's worth of responsibility. He wasn't looking forward to more.

"What do you want us to do?" Javi asked, not really wanting to hear the answer.

"Oh, the regular things. Make your beds and keep your rooms neat, pick up your toys, and clean up after yourselves when you're in other parts of the house. Javier, you can help Nico at first, but he'll learn fast. You'll see. You can help me with the cooking sometimes, and we'll alternate days when we wash dishes. Nico can help you."

As Amparo went on listing different chores—taking out the trash, gardening, walking Fidel—Javi grew more and more tense. His fists clenched and unclenched.

With all these chores, when would he have time for himself?

"And we'll have to set some ground rules." Amparo looked pointedly at Nico, who was inspecting a button in the sofa cushion. "Nicolás?"

Nico looked up and gave her a bright smile, as if to say he'd been listening all along.

Amparo cleared her throat. "Nicolás, you may not leave the house without telling someone—Javier or me—okay? And when a family member is looking for you, you must not continue playing hide-and-seek."

Amparo lifted an eyebrow. Nico nodded happily.

Apparently satisfied that Nico understood, Amparo went on to list other ground rules: daily number of hours watching unsupervised television, daily number of hours watching supervised television (she seemed to feel that a certain amount of television viewing during the summer would help the boys with their English), required number of hours reading English (this was for Javi's benefit), number of hours on the phone (as if Javi had anyone to talk to). There were other rules on the list, but Javi stopped listening. He was sure his aunt would remind him of anything he "forgot."

As Amparo continued to talk and the boys continued to pretend to listen—Nico now playing with ZsaZsa's tail and Javi staring out the window—the shadows in the room deepened. The gloom seemed to seep into Javi's pores. Flashes of his old life whizzed through his mind. But Javi tried not to concentrate on any one memory too long. The contrast between then and now was too painful.

When she was done with her speech, Amparo took the boys to see their room.

As they climbed the stairs, she told them, "I'm afraid you'll have to share a room until I can find a new place to store my old books and free up the guest room. The house has four bedrooms and a den, but somehow I've managed to fill all the spare rooms with my books and boxes."

When she opened the door, Javi noticed he would be sharing the room with more than his brother. One wall was lined to the ceiling with shelves packed with Amparo's boxes. It looked like a storage room. Tucked in the corner, against the opposite wall, stood two twin beds stacked one on top of the other.

"I hope you don't mind bunk beds. It was the best I could do with the small amount of space."

Javi glanced around the rest of the room. The wall across from where they had entered held a picture window. Despite the large window, the tall pines that shaded the backyard kept the room as dark and gloomy as the rest of the house. From the window, Javi could see the footbridge, the tiny creek, and the woods beyond. The wall next to the hall door was mostly a large closet.

"I did manage to clear the closet, so you have it all to yourselves."

The closet door yawned open, exposing a large walk-in space. Javi stared at the closet. In this large house, all that would be his and Nico's was this closet and half of a small room. He remembered his old bedroom, so bright and spacious. Even little Nico had had a large, sunny room.

Well, so much for belonging and being made to feel at home. He felt like a stray animal a family takes in and clears a tiny spot for in the garage or laundry room or storage room. They don't go to too much trouble since they are only taking in the stray for a little while ... until they can find a suitable home for it. After all, a stray won't know the difference. And shouldn't it be grateful for any small shelter to keep it safe?

Was this what was happening? Was their aunt secretly hoping that some other relative would step forward and take the boys? In the meantime she'd have done her duty, fed them, kept them safe and warm, and at the same time not really gone to too much trouble—

"Javier? As soon as I've finished grading the last term papers and exams, I'll have time to go shopping with you. We'll spend the summer getting this room ready for Nicolás and decorating the room next door for you. Okay?"

"No matter," he muttered.

"Of course it matters. I'll be done in another week or so, then I'll be all yours."

"You no need to *engañarme*. I know what is happening."

"I'm not trying to fool you. Javier? Look at me."

Amparo took his shoulders and turned him toward her. Javi scowled and looked away, shrugging his shoulders free of her grasp. No matter what she said, she wasn't going to fool him. He could feel the tears threatening again and willed them away. He didn't need her. Neither did Nico. Nico had him. He'd take care of them both.

Javi clenched his fists and pushed his lips into a straight, tight line. For the first time since the accident, Javi felt angry at his parents for dying and leaving him and Nico alone. For taking away the perfect family life, the perfect home—

A sudden shudder, followed by something that felt like a rolling wave, shook the walls. On the top shelf a precariously positioned box rattled and fell to the floor with a loud *crash!* Nico, who had been gazing out the window, yelped and darted to Javi's side, burying his head in his brother's chest.

Amparo knelt beside the boys and gave Javi a reassuring squeeze on the shoulder. "It's okay, *muchachos*," she said with a nervous little laugh. "That was just a small earthquake. Welcome to California."

SLOWLY JAVI OPENED HIS EYES. The room was dark and unfamiliar. Moonlight spilled through the window, bathing the walls and furniture in an eerie glow. It took him a few moments to remember where he was.

Something had wakened him. He vaguely remembered someone crying out his name . . . Nico!

Javi peered over the side of his bed to the bunk below. He blinked. The bed was empty, the covers pulled back.

His gaze slid to the window. The moon illuminated the wooden bridge. Just beyond the bridge, an old oak stretched its twisted limbs. That was where he'd felt the evil presence yesterday. Beyond the oak the woods waited, dark and sinister.

A shiver wriggled up his spine. Nico was out there, in those woods.

Javi leaped from the upper bunk and raced down the

stairs and into the backyard. It wasn't until his feet touched the moist grass that he realized he was barefoot.

He darted across the bridge, pausing for only a moment to glance at the old oak. In that instant he heard the cry again.

"Javi! Help me, Javi. I'm frightened!"

It was Nico's voice. Javi turned left at the bridge and crashed into the woods, following his brother's cries. The deeper he ran into the woods, the darker they got. Brambles and undergrowth ripped at his pajama bottoms; wooden fingers clawed his face and arms and grabbed his hair.

He held out his arms to protect his face and pumped his legs in rhythm to his heart. He couldn't worry about the burning in his lungs or the stitch in his side—he had to follow the voice, he had to find his brother. But Nico's cries were louder now, so loud they seemed to fill the night. Their shrillness vibrated his bones and shot through his nerves. He stumbled and fell on a carpet of dry pine needles.

"Javi! Help me!"

Nico's screams almost shattered Javi's eardrums. He reached out blindly, thinking Nico must be near.

Something cold, cold, cold grabbed Javi's arms and dragged him through the pine needles. All the while, Nico's screams cut through the darkness and into his heart.

Javi kicked his legs, trying to wrap them around a tree trunk or a bush, something to help him pull free of the thing that was dragging him. The more he struggled, the stronger the thing seemed to become.

All at once the dragging stopped, and the coldness slithered down his arms and enveloped his entire body. He was smothering in an icy fog.

Abruptly his breathing stopped, and he descended into blackness.

Javi awoke in the upper bunk, his heart still pounding. It was morning, cool and foggy. He leaned over the side of his bed. Nico slept contentedly, his arm wrapped around Pulito, his floppy stuffed dog.

A dream. It had all been a dream.

Javi lay back on his pillow and closed his eyes, remembering another dream, one that had seemed as real as this one felt. It came the night before his parents' accident. He had dreamed that the next day his parents would visit Papi's sick aunt Vela, as they often did, but this time they would not return. A drunk driver would ram the center divide on the highway that took them to the hospital and crash into them, head-on. Their car would be squashed like a soda can.

The dream had felt so real, he knew he had to warn them. But when he did, Mami had hugged him and told him not to worry. Papi had smiled sympathetically but said it was only a nightmare after all, and nightmares didn't come true.

But that one had.

And so might the one he'd had last night.

"I see you're an early riser," Amparo said when Javi padded into the kitchen.

Fidel greeted him with a wag of his tail and a short bark. Amparo smiled and motioned for him to sit.

"How did you sleep?"

Javi shrugged. "Fine," he lied, remembering the nightmare. And he was still worried about Nico and his imaginary friend.

"How's Nicolás?"

"Still asleep."

"He'll be all right, Javier. Give him time."

"I not know. That name. How Nico think of such a name?"

"Maybe he made it up."

Javi considered that. "Nico make up many names—for his toys. But they always sound make up, like Pulito, the name of his stuffed dog. They sound like *disparates.*"

"Like nonsense."

He nodded. "But this name . . . I never hear such a name. It sound very real—no nonsense."

"*Hmm* . . . did it? I don't remember . . ."

"I remember. I never forget such a name—Hamish Brenden McTavish." Javi carefully enunciated each syllable.

"It does sound real. Scottish, I think."

Amparo glanced at Javi. Worry lines etched his forehead. She sighed. "Look, Javier, I will grant you it is an unusual name. But Nicolás is an intelligent little boy. Both of you are very bright. He probably heard it on the plane or in the airport and remembered it."

Javi nodded. That was true. It was possible that Nico had heard the name at the airport. There had been a lot of commotion around them during the trip. Large groups of people coming and going, milling about, talking. Names had been called. Javi himself was so absorbed in his own thoughts, he hadn't paid much attention to what was happening around them. But Nico might have been listening.

Javi relaxed and took a chair across from Amparo.

"Hungry?" she asked. "I can make scrambled eggs or cereal."

Javi glanced at her bowl. "What . . . you eat?"

"Granola and milk with bananas."

Javi brightened. "Bananas? You have?"

"Sure. I can even get mangoes and papayas, if you start to crave tropical fruits. So, what would you like?"

"You can make *tortilla de guineo*?"

Amparo's smile faded. "Banana omelet? Well . . . *hmm-mm* . . . banana omelet . . ."

Javi felt his face burn. "It is all right. It is too much trouble—"

"No, Javier, it's not that, it's just—"

"I have milk and a banana."

"Javier, let me explain. I've never been much of a cook. Living alone, I've gotten used to cooking simple things. And eating out a lot."

Javi nodded. "I understand."

"But that doesn't mean I'm not willing to learn new recipes, I'm just saying I may not know many of the recipes your mami cooked. And I may need your help . . . and patience."

Javi shrugged. "It is all right, really."

Amparo pushed back her chair and opened the refrigerator. "Okay. Eggs, bananas—anything else for a banana omelet?"

"Milk, I think."

"Milk." Amparo grabbed the milk, eggs, and bananas and placed them next to a big bowl and a wooden spoon. "Now what?"

"Mami smash the bananas with a fork. Then she . . . batter . . . the eggs?" Javi glanced at Amparo.

"She beat the eggs?"

"*Sí*, and she add bananas and milk."

"That's not so hard. I can do that." Amparo grabbed a plate and began to mash two bananas. "Like this, you think?"

Javi stepped to the counter. "I think that . . . yes."

"Now, how many eggs—two, three?"

Javi looked down at the floor and shook his head.

"That's okay. We'll guess. Three, I think. If it's too much, Nicolás can have the rest. Now, how about milk? Two tablespoons sounds right. How about vanilla? Did she use vanilla?"

Javi shrugged a shoulder.

"Well, it can't hurt. Just a touch." Amparo mashed the concoction around the bowl with the wooden spoon. "Now what? How did your mami cook the omelet? Griddle? Frying pan?" Amparo held up both items for Javi's examination.

"This one." Javi pointed at the large frying pan.

"Oil or butter?"

Javi bit his lip, thinking, remembering. Suddenly he realized how much it meant to him to do this right. To bring back a little bit of his mother. "Oil, I think—no, butter. Yes, butter."

"Butter it is." Amparo melted a pat of butter in the big frying pan. When the pan was coated, she poured in the banana-egg mixture.

Javi almost held his breath as he watched the gloppy yellow mixture bubble.

"You know, Javier . . . Javi"—Amparo cupped Javi's chin in her hand and lifted his face so they were looking into each other's eyes—"it's okay if the omelet doesn't come out just right the first few times. Like I said, I'm not a very good cook, so I might mess it up. But I'll make you a deal. I'll call your Tití Luisa tonight and have her send me all your mami's favorite recipes. Then you and I can try them together."

Javi shrugged and walked back to the table to wait. The sweet, buttery smell reminded him of the last time he'd watched his mother bustle about the kitchen, humming as she prepared a banana omelet.

Maybe they'd done it right. Maybe it would taste the same. It smelled the same.

When the omelet was done, his aunt slid it onto a large plate. "A little big, isn't it?" She cut off half, pushed it onto another plate, and set it in front of Javi. "I'll keep the rest warm for Nico."

Javi cut into the omelet with his fork. It oozed over the top and was burnt on the bottom. The inside was much more runny than the omelets his mother used to make, but it tasted okay. It just wasn't what he had been craving.

A lump formed in his throat.

"How is it?" Amparo's eyes glowed expectantly.

Javi didn't want to be rude. She had tried.

"Fine," he said. "It is fine."

"Good," she said. "And next time it'll be better. I promise."

Javi nodded. But it would never be the same.

Nothing would ever be the same.

8

"HURRY, JAVI," SAID AMPARO, hustling the boys into the garage. "I have a lot to do this afternoon." She was dropping Javi off at Willo's house, then taking Nico with her to the university, where she would be working in her office.

As Javi tugged Nico behind him, leading him around the car, Nico kept holding back and gesturing to something behind them.

"I'm trying, Tití," Javi replied in Spanish, "but Nico seems to have forgotten something. What is it, Nico? Did you misplace Pulito again?"

"I've got Pulito right here." Amparo held up the bedraggled stuffed dog.

Javi pointed. "See, Nico? There he is—hurry up."

But Nico kept pulling back and gesturing.

Javi opened the back door. "Come on, Nico!"

Nico crawled onto the backseat, but he kept looking

out the side window. Javi clipped the seat belt around Nico, then slid in beside him.

"Everyone set?" Amparo called from the front.

Javi glanced at his brother. The corners of the little boy's mouth were curved down. "I think Nico wants Pulito."

Amparo handed the stuffed dog to Javi and turned on the ignition. As the car backed out of the garage, Nico squirmed in his seat.

"Now what's wrong?" Javi asked.

"Hamish can't come with us."

"Hamish? Oh, your new friend." Javi rolled his eyes.

Amparo stopped the car. "It's okay if Hamish comes along. I don't mind. Ask him to come."

"I already asked him to come," said Nico, beginning to whine, "but he said he can't. He'll be all alone."

"He'll be all right," Javi said. "He was okay before you met him, right?"

Nico shook his head. "He was afraid. And now he's afraid again."

Javi got an idea. "Don't worry. Tell him to go in the house and play with Fidel. He likes Fidel, doesn't he? That way he won't be alone."

Nico nodded and opened the side window. He leaned out and whispered something.

"Hurry, Nico, it's getting late," Amparo said.

Nico closed the window. He smiled. "Hamish said he will stay with Fidel."

Amparo gave a satisfied grunt and started the car again, easing it along the bumpy gravel drive before anything else interrupted their trip.

Javi leaned back in his seat. He didn't like the idea of

an imaginary friend. It made him feel . . . creepy. Yes, that was a good word—creepy. But he didn't say anything more about it. If his aunt thought it was all right, then it must be. After all, she was a trained psychologist.

But he still felt creepy.

"Nicolás will be fine with me, Javi. Don't worry," Amparo said when they pulled up to Willo's house. "I'll be back around three. Have fun."

Reluctantly Javi slid out of the car. Before closing the door he took a long look at his little brother, who gazed back at him over Pulito's head.

Waving good-bye, Amparo backed up the car and drove away.

As he watched the black Volvo disappear behind the trees, Javi began to wish he'd elected to go with Amparo and Nico. He didn't want to spend the afternoon with a girl he hardly knew. A strange and annoying girl. He also didn't like having a friendship forced on him. He preferred picking his own friends—boys his own age.

"Just in time!"

Javi turned. Willo was coming out of the garage, pushing a bicycle. Another bicycle was already waiting in the driveway.

"I'm starving," she said, straddling one of the bikes. "I thought we could ride to town and have lunch. My treat this time—since you're new and all. Then I can show you around."

Javi glanced at the bike beside her.

"Yes, this is for you. Daddy's bike. He said I should lend it to you until Amparo gets you your own. He hasn't had much time to ride lately. Finals and all."

Javi strode over to the bike. With heavy, rough tires and

straight handlebars, it was different from the sleek racing bikes he was used to.

"Ready?" Willo asked.

Javi straddled the bike and coasted down the driveway. Willo quickly caught up and led the way down the winding woodsy road.

It was an enchanted place, both beautiful and ominous. Warm, dry air whisked by, carrying the scent of pines and weeds and strange forest smells that were alien to Javi. Shafts of sunlight slanted through the heavy canopy of branches, creating dancing patterns of light and shadow on the road.

Above them, birds—mockingbirds, he found out later—called to each other in odd shrieks that sounded almost human, a screechy, garbled foreign language. At one point a deer darted to the edge of the road and, on seeing them, froze for an instant, then darted back into the woods, disappearing almost as quickly as it had appeared.

All too soon the woods fell away, and they were riding along the outskirts of a suburb. Large houses, small houses, all arranged in neat rows along clean streets that spiraled around the side of a hill.

The road took a tight curve and made a steep descent that coasted them into town. Javi followed Willo, staying on a specially marked bicycle path alongside the city traffic. She turned at a side street and slid to a stop. The smell of burgers and fries made Javi's mouth water. He was hungrier than he'd thought.

"Here," said Willo, "we'll chain our bikes to this pole. The restaurant is right next door."

Willo led him past the hamburger joint to a Mediterranean deli.

"Why here?" Javi asked, gazing longingly at the burger joint. "The hamburgers are next door."

Willo shuddered. "Ugh! You don't want meat all the time, do you? Try something new. Ever taste a falafel?"

"It's not poison, Javi," Willo said, grinning. "Try it, it's really good."

Javi stared at the tray before him. In a red plastic basket lined with wax paper, a flat, round bread, sliced at one edge, was filled to bursting with shredded lettuce, a tan-colored glop, and a few balls that looked deep-fried. On the side was something that looked like grain mixed with parsley, green onions, and tomatoes.

Willo snorted. "Look, you eat it like this."

She picked up her sandwich and bit into the open end. White goo dripped down the side of her mouth. She giggled and dabbed at it with a napkin, both cheeks plump with food.

Javi scowled at his falafel, then, pretending it was a burger, he took a large bite. Goo dripped down the side of his mouth, too. He chewed tentatively. It wasn't bad. It tasted like something his mother used to make, but he couldn't remember what.

Willo laughed. "See, not bad." She reached out to wipe the side of his face. "California is a great place to get vegetarian cuisine. This is a good welcome-to-California meal for you."

"I am already welcome to California."

" 'I *was* already wel*comed* to California'—past tense." Willo paused. "You were? How was that?"

"The earth shook for us."

Willo looked puzzled. "You mean an earthquake?"

Javi nodded.

"Really? When?"

"Yesterday, after you leave."

"After I *left*—past tense. Must have been a little one. I didn't feel anything. Didn't hear about it on the news, either."

"Tití Amparo say it small, also. But to Nico and me, it feel too large. It make a box fall."

"The first time can be scary." Willo sipped her lemonade. "Some people are always frightened by them, no matter how small. Mom used to hate earthquakes. I've never felt a real big one."

Javi didn't want to admit how much the earthquake had frightened him. He picked up his sandwich and continued eating.

"Why do you call Amparo 'Tití'?" Willo asked.

"It mean 'Auntie,' " Javi replied, glad to be the one providing information for once.

"I've got an idea. In exchange for helping you improve your English, you can teach me Spanish."

Javi considered her offer. "You wish to learn Spanish?"

"Sure, why not? I like learning things. And I plan to take Spanish in junior high. It'll give me a head start."

"If you like," he said with a shrug.

Willo stuck out her hand. "Deal, then."

Javi glanced at her hand. It seemed he had a friend whether he wanted one or not. He sighed, wiped his hand, and grasped hers.

"Deal, then."

9

"I NEED SOME MORE BOOKS. Let's stop at the library," Willo said after she'd given Javi a tour of most of the downtown area.

As they stepped into the cool, dark building, Willo whispered, "*Shh-hh.* Let's go this way, to avoid the front desk. I don't want to run into—"

"Willo! How delightful to see you," said a shrill female voice.

Willo's face scrunched up into a sour grimace, but when she turned to meet the speaker, it had changed to an expression of innocence.

"Hello, Ms. Watkins," Willo said with a tight smile.

Javi turned. A short woman with long, frizzy red hair and a pale complexion was smiling adoringly at Willo. She seemed to have been poured into a tiny orange minidress that made her look like a walking carrot.

Ms. Watkins shook her red hair. "And how is your father? It's been so long since he's come to the library."

"He usually uses the libraries at Cal—since he works there and all. And I'm old enough to ride my bike through town, so he doesn't need to drive me anymore."

Ms. Watkins's smile faded. "Oh, what a shame." She twirled a strand of hair with her finger as she took in the disappointing news. Then she brightened. "Listen, Willo, tell him if he ever needs some research done, I'm always available."

"Sure, but he has research assistants, you know."

Ms. Watkins stared at her. After a few seconds her face broke into an eager smile. "But I'm available for emergencies. If he ever gets stuck and needs some quick research, tell him to call me."

"Sure, okay, I'll tell him." As she spoke, Willo pushed Javi sideways, away from Ms. Watkins. "We'll see you later . . ."

Ms. Watkins reached out and took Willo's arm. "But you haven't introduced me to your new friend."

Willo turned to Javi and crossed her eyes. "I'm sorry. Ms. Watkins, this is Javi Leál, Amparo's nephew. He and his little brother are going to be living with her from now on. Javi, this is Ms. Watkins, one of the librarians."

"So you're Dr. Leál's nephew." Ms. Watkins's lips screwed up into a wrinkled prune. "Glad to meet you."

Javi grasped her extended hand. It felt like a chunk of cold ham. "Glad to meet you, also."

"Isn't that delightful! You have an accent. Where are you from, Mexico?"

Javi's jaw tightened. He didn't like her tone. "No, I am from Puerto Rico."

Ms. Watkins's eyebrows snapped up. "Really? You don't look Puerto Rican. I lived in New York for a few years, and—"

"We really have to hurry, Ms. Watkins," said Willo, pulling Javi. "I need to pick up some books, then we have to get home."

"Yes, of course."

Willo yanked Javi's arm. "Hurry," she whispered.

They had almost disappeared around the corner when they heard Ms. Watkins's voice. "Willo?"

Willo and Javi froze. Willo's grasp on Javi's arm tightened.

"Willo, dear"—Ms. Watkins stepped around to face them—"I almost forgot to tell you. We've started a new summer reading program at the library. Perhaps you and Javi would like to participate?"

"Well, I don't know . . ."

"It's truly exciting. I know your father will approve. We'd like some of the best readers from our middle grades to help the children's librarian select new books. It's an experiment, so we want to keep the group small. Each child will be lent advance reading samples of new books that publishers have sent to Ms. Snow. Then you will all meet in a group and critique the books and give her a recommendation. What do you think—would you and Javi like to participate?"

Willo glanced at Javi. "Sounds interesting, but we'll need to talk about it."

Ms. Watkins handed them each a flyer. "Here's the information on the program. If you want to participate, you'll need to fill out the attached form and submit it as soon as possible. There will be only six participants. Ms. Snow will make the final selection, but since we're looking for responsible young people, you will be perfect, Willo . . . And you, too, Javi."

"Thanks, Ms. Watkins. Javi and I will discuss it. Come on, Javi, let's get the books."

They left Ms. Watkins standing in the middle of the hall, looking like a bewildered carrot that someone had stuck upright in the earth.

"Hurry, Javi." Willo pulled Javi into the stacks. "Let's disappear before she gets another chance to stop us."

"I not know why, but I think I not like that woman."

Willo snorted. "I know why. She's a royal pain, that's why. Daddy can't *stand* her."

"But I think that Ms. Watkins can stand your father too much."

Willo crossed her eyes again and made a silly face. "No kidding! The woman's crazy about him. It's so embarrassing. I'm surprised she didn't give me her home phone number to take to him—just for emergencies."

"She not seem to like Tití Amparo very much."

"She *did* not seem," Willo corrected. "Well, of course not. She thinks Amparo and Daddy are an item."

"A what?"

"An item. It means that they are girlfriend and boyfriend."

Javi's eyes opened wide. "They are *novios?*"

"If *novios* means what I think it means, no. They're just friends. They were friends when Mom was still alive. But Ms. Watkins is jealous of any woman who can get Daddy's attention."

Willo began to choose a few books. They looked a lot more ambitious than anything Javi had ever tried.

"Hey, look." Willo pulled a thick book from the shelf. "This looks interesting. *Unsolved Mysteries of the Twentieth Century.* I love this kind of thing."

Javi eyed the thick book. "It appear very difficult."

"But, look"—Willo fanned the pages—"it's divided into short stories about different unsolved mysteries. Each story is only a few pages long. That's not so bad."

Javi flipped through the pages. "Perhaps it is not so bad. *Me gusta*—it give me pleasure—the unsolved mystery."

"You mean you *like* unsolved mysteries."

"Yes, I like unsolved mysteries too much."

"*Very* much."

"*Ah,*" Javi replied, trying to remember all she was teaching him, "*very* much. Perhaps I can read *algunos*—some?"—Willo nodded—"some stories."

"Great! I'll check it out for you, then I'll read it when you're done."

As Willo turned to choose a few more books, Javi scanned the shelves. He spotted a thin book entitled *Ghostly Tales from the Crypt.* He pulled it out. It had large type and short stories.

"Willo, may you check this out for me, also?"

Willo grinned. "Sure. Looks like we have the same taste in books. I read that one last year." She crossed her eyes and gave a mock shudder. "*Muy* scarioso!"

"What about the reading program?" Javi asked when Willo had finished choosing her books. He held up his flyer.

"Oh yeah, I almost forgot." Willo quickly scanned her flyer. "This might be really good for you, Javi. They'll have lots of middle-grade mysteries, and by the end of the summer you can graduate to young adult books."

"You not—*did* not like?"

" '*Do* not like'—present tense." Willo shrugged. "I'm not much of a joiner. I don't like groups. But don't let that stop you."

Javi shrugged, too. He didn't like the idea of joining a group of strange kids, either. He was just starting to get used to Willo.

Willo grabbed their books, and they took them to the loan desk. After Willo checked out the books, they headed for the door.

"Oh, Willo . . ."

The shrill voice froze the pair in their tracks.

Slowed down by her high heels and tight skirt, Ms. Watkins ran toward them with tiny mincing steps. She flapped a piece of paper above her head. "I just wanted to give you my home phone number. You know, in case your dad has an emergency."

Without a word Willo grabbed the piece of paper, and she and Javi ran outside, where they burst into wild peals of laughter.

"JAVI, DID YOU BRING HOME THIS FLYER?"

Amparo poked her head into the family room, where Javi and Nico were watching a *National Geographic* special on the plight of the tiger. ZsaZsa and Misifú were curled together at the end of the couch. Fidel sprawled between the boys, his head on Nico's lap.

Amparo held up the flyer on the summer reading program.

Javi nodded. "Willo take"—he paused, remembering Willo's voice saying "past tense"—"*took* me to the library. Ms. Watkins give—gave us one each."

"It looks like a great program. Did you sign up?"

"No," he said, looking back at the screen.

Amparo muted the sound. "You didn't? Why not?"

"*No conozco a nadie* —"

"English, please, Javi."

Javi sighed and began again. "I do not know anyone who will participate."

"You know Willo."

"Willo do not—does not—wish to join."

"She would if you asked her to. Anyway, you need to meet other kids your age. And it will help with your English."

"Willo help with my English. And I help with her Spanish—we make a deal." Javi felt himself tensing. This was not a conversation he wanted to be having. His gaze slid back to the TV screen. Maybe his aunt would get the hint.

Amparo sat on the coffee table in front of Javi, blocking his view. "It's more than just speaking English. You need to practice reading English so it comes easily."

Javi looked down at his hands. He pulled on a hangnail, tugging till it hurt. "I practice reading English by myself," he muttered. "I choose my own books."

"Javi, the books you will be exposed to in this program are excellent books. I know you'll enjoy them and benefit from the experience."

Javi clenched his jaw. His breathing felt strained, heavy. "But this is my summer vacation . . ." His voice sounded whiny. He bit his lip, trying to control unwanted tears.

Amparo leaned forward and gently stroked his hair. "Javi, I know it's your vacation, but this is important. And it'll be fun. Give it a chance. I'll talk to Ms. Snow and make sure you're selected, then I'll ask Willo—"

"No!" Javi jerked away from her and stood up.

He glared at his aunt. Hot tears finally fell. In his frustration, he slipped back into Spanish. "You treat me like a baby. I can talk to Willo. I can choose my own friends!" His voice cracked, humiliating him further.

"Javi, please . . . you have to trust me to know what's best—"

"You don't know what's best! You don't know me!"

At that moment the sound from the TV set came on, blaring a heavy-metal tune. It was set to the top of the volume control.

Amparo jumped from her seat as if she'd been burned. Nico's hands flew up to his ears. He scrunched his eyes shut. ZsaZsa darted from the room; Misifú hunched her back and hissed, while Fidel barked at the TV set.

Javi's heart pounded to the beat of the heavy-metal guitar. He brushed aside angry tears.

They stared at the screen. The television was now set to MTV—a few minutes before, it had been on PBS.

"*Shh-hh*, Fidel!" With trembling hands, Amparo lifted the remote control and turned off the TV. Her face was pale and her eyes wide. She held a hand to her heart. Sinking onto the couch, she stared at the blank screen. "What—what was that?"

Javi fought the desire to comfort his aunt. He was not yet ready to forgive her. And for the moment, he refused to speak English. "You don't know? I thought you knew everything."

Amparo's head snapped toward Javi. She looked as if he had slapped her. Instantly he wished he could snatch back the words. He wished he could bring himself to go to her, to tell her he was sorry, but something held him back.

Amparo shook her head sadly. "Javi, please don't make things more difficult than they need to be. I'm trying—"

Javi couldn't stand to hear any more. He turned and bolted from the room. He felt more confused than he had ever felt. Opposite emotions waged a tug-of-war. His insides bubbled with shame and anger, guilt and self-righteousness, love and hate.

He seemed to be losing control—control of his emotions, control of his words, control of his life. He was on a carousel, spinning wildly, and he couldn't get off.

Javi lay on his bed, headphones over his ears, listening to one of his favorite bands and staring at the ceiling. The sunny afternoon had turned cool and gloomy. Fog had rolled in, and with it came shadows. But he was in no mood to turn on a light.

At first he had been too upset and confused to wonder about what had happened in the family room. But now he wondered—in fact, he couldn't erase the scene from his mind.

He and Nico had been watching the special on tigers when Amparo had come in to talk to him. She had muted the sound, but she hadn't changed the channel. Had she?

No, he distinctly remembered seeing a man empty a burlap bag full of tiger bones onto the ground. He remembered wishing his aunt would leave so he could listen to what the narrator was saying. Javi had been outraged at the cruelty of poachers and at the waste of such majestic creatures for the sake of money. At that very moment, Amparo had sat down in front of him, blocking his view.

Maybe she sat on the remote control. Or maybe she inadvertently touched it when they were arguing, changing the channel and increasing the volume. He knew that simply adjusting the volume would unmute the sound.

That had to be it. What other explanation was there? TV sets don't switch channels and increase volume on their own. And it hadn't been Nico. He hadn't moved from

Javi's side on the couch since the documentary had started.

Nico's giggles made Javi remove his earphones and look down. Nico was kneeling on the floor in front of a wooden stool. On the stool lay seashells, plastic coins, and paper play money.

Nico held out a large pink conch and turned it slowly, showing all its sides. He seemed to be displaying it for someone's examination. Then he set it down and began counting paper money.

"*Uno, dos, tres—hmm-mm?*" Nico tilted his head, listening. Then he nodded. "Okay. One, two, three, *cuatro, cinco—¿Como?*" He listened again. "Four . . . five, six, seven . . . eight, nine . . . ten . . ."

Nico continued counting until he reached twenty. With each number he set down a bill, until he had counted twenty bills.

As Javi watched, tiny shivers shimmied down his spine to the backs of his legs.

"Nico, where did you learn to count in English? You didn't know how this morning when Tití Amparo asked you. You can barely count to twenty in Spanish."

Nico beamed and pointed at the air in front of him. "Hamish taught me."

11

AT DINNER THAT NIGHT Javi had even more reason to feel ashamed for the way he had treated his aunt. Amparo had made *arroz y habichuelas,* Puerto Rican–style rice and beans. He knew how much of an effort it must have been with all the other work she had to do. Yet she had gone out of her way to cook an old familiar favorite to make the boys feel welcome.

Maybe he was wrong about his aunt. Maybe she wasn't just waiting until some other relative showed up who would take them off her hands. Still, he couldn't quite bring himself to apologize. He wasn't happy about having to participate in the reading program, and he didn't want her to start thinking he was.

Also, it was so hard to express his true feelings in English. He fumbled about, struggling for the right words to convey emotions he could barely express even in his native language. Even with easy topics, he was still thinking in Spanish, then translating his thoughts to English. Why couldn't she see how hard all this was for him? Why couldn't she give him a break?

"Javi? What would you like on your salad?" Amparo stood beside him with two bottles of salad dressing. "Italian or Thousand Island?"

"Italian."

Amparo handed him the bottle, then took her seat at the head of the table. Javi and Nico sat on either side of her. Javi spooned some white rice onto his plate. Over that he ladled some beans. Amparo served Nico and herself.

They began eating in silence. Javi wished he could think of something to say to cut the tension. The room was so quiet he could hear himself swallow. He could even hear his muscles creak.

Amparo cleared her throat. "How's the rice?"

Javi had started with his salad. He took a bite of rice and beans. The rice was crunchy and dry. The beans were hard and too salty.

"Good," he lied.

Amparo gave a nervous giggle. "I was afraid I undercooked the rice. It stays hard on the inside when you undercook it."

She took a forkful of rice and beans. She chewed. Javi looked away. He heard her swallow. He looked up. Her face had the expression of someone who has just realized she swallowed a bug.

Their eyes met.

Amparo sucked in her lips and pressed them together; her eyes widened. As she and Javi stared at each other, a rasping sound, like a snort, escaped from behind Amparo's pressed lips. At the same time, a bubble of giggles erupted from Javi's throat. They burst into laughter.

Nico joined in the laughter, obviously laughing just to laugh, not because he knew why they were laughing. He swung his legs happily and took a bite of rice and beans.

"Mm-mm," he said, as he crunched the undercooked rice, *"pega'o!"*

Amparo and Javi looked at each other and roared. *Pega'o* is the slang term for *pegado,* which is the crunchy golden-brown rice that sometimes sticks to the bottom of the pot. Javi and Nico would always beg for *pega'o,* so their mother tried to overcook part of the rice to make sure everyone, including their dad, had some *pega'o.*

"I'm sorry, Javi," said Amparo, between giggles. "I'll have to keep trying."

They began to eat in silence again, but this time the silence was comfortable. Javi's mind wandered back to his trip to the library with Willo.

"Tití, how do I look?"

Amparo looked up, puzzled, and studied Javi's face. "You look fine. Why?" She reached over and felt his forehead. "Do you feel sick?"

"No, I mean like who do I look?"

"Who do you look like?"

Javi nodded.

"Well, I suppose you have your mami's blue eyes and her nose, and you definitely have your papi's wonderful head of hair and shape of the face. Our side of the family has that widow's peak and dimpled chin."

"No, I do not mean who in the family. I mean, do I look Puerto Rican?"

Amparo's back stiffened. "Why would you ask that?"

"At the library, me and Willo—*o sea*, Willo and I—met a lady. Ms. Watkins. She say I do not look Puerto Rican."

Amparo's lips tightened. "Bambi Watkins wears her skirts too tight, and it affects the blood flow to her brain."

"What?"

"Never mind. Don't pay any attention to what that woman says. Just be polite to her, and when she speaks, keep in mind that she is a very small person."

Javi puzzled over his aunt's words. "She is very small, but I do not understand. I must not listen to people who are not very tall?"

Amparo smiled and shook her head. "No, on the contrary. I was not referring to her physical size, her height—*su altura*. I don't even mean the size of her brain. I mean the size of her heart and her mind. Some people are very narrow-minded—they don't think before they speak, or afterward, either. Some people just don't think very much."

Javi nodded. "I think I understand. She seem not very nice. I do not like the way she speak to me. Willo and her father do not like her."

"That's the understatement of the year," Amparo mumbled under her breath. To Javi, she added, "Don't worry about how you look. You look exactly as any eleven-year-old boy should look."

"Nico, are you tired of watching?" Javi asked, when after only half an hour of watching television, Nico began to fidget. "I thought you liked movies about cats."

Nico pulled Javi close and whispered in his ear, "Hamish wants to play."

"Oh, it's Hamish who wants to play, is it? Well, I want to

see the rest of this movie, so why don't you go play with Hamish?"

Nico slid off the couch, pulling Fidel, who had been thumping his tail against Javi's leg, with him. He ran off to play, and Fidel trotted after him.

"Nico," Javi called before he disappeared into the hall, "no hide-and-seek."

After the movie was over, Javi began to wonder how Nico was doing. In a way he was glad that Nico wasn't always pestering him to play or to keep him entertained. He seemed to be getting more independent. But at the same time, Javi still didn't like the idea that what was entertaining Nico was an imaginary friend. There was something strange about how Nico was suddenly learning to count, learning English, and learning to be more independent. All because of a friend he had created himself.

Before heading upstairs, Javi stopped in to see if Nico was playing in the den. When he walked in, he found his aunt immersed in grading term papers.

"Tití, you see Nico?" Javi asked.

"No," Amparo replied absently, still reading the paper in her hand, "but I thought I heard him bouncing his ball upstairs. Weren't you guys watching TV?" Amparo put the paper down and looked up at Javi.

"We watch, but he become, *uh . . . aburrido . . .* bored?"

Amparo nodded.

"I stay and watch the rest."

" '*Became* bored. *Stayed* and *watched* the rest.' Your English vocabulary is improving, Javi. I'm very pleased. Now you need to work on your tenses—past, present, and future."

Javi sighed. "Tenses, *sí*, I try." He remembered Willo

correcting his tenses—past, present, future, past, present—
¡Basta, basta ya! Enough, already!

Amparo checked her watch. "It's getting kind of late. Are you heading for bed?"

"Yes, as soon as I find Nico." He paused, searching for the right words. "Tití? Something strange happen—happened—before dinner."

"Oh, what was that?"

"Nico is playing—selling seashells and counting money paper—"

"Paper money?"

"Yes, paper money—and he count to twenty. Perfectly. In English."

"I thought he said he didn't know how to count in English."

"He cannot even count to twenty in Spanish. Not without mistakes."

"I don't understand."

"He say—said—Hamish teach him."

Amparo frowned. "Well, there must be a logical explanation. He probably learned this morning while he was watching television."

"He did not watch this morning. We did not have time."

Amparo stared at Javi. After a few seconds she shook her head. "I'm sure there's a logical explanation. Don't worry about it. Nico is simply picking up things more quickly than we expected. That's a good thing, not something to worry about. So why don't you find Nico and help him get ready for bed?"

"*Bendición*, Tití." Javi leaned down and kissed her cheek.

"God bless you, *m'ijo*," she said, kissing him back. "I'll be in to check on you in half an hour or so."

As Javi climbed the stairs, he wasn't so sure there was a logical explanation for Nico's strange behavior. If there was, what was it?

When Javi entered the bedroom, he found Nico sitting spread legged on the floor, facing the bunk beds. He was rolling a large ball under the lower bunk, and without hitting the far wall, the ball was rolling back to him.

"Nico, did you teach Fidel to return the ball to you like that?"

Nico looked up and grinned. He shook his head.

Javi knelt beside the bed. "So who's rolling the ball back? Misifú?"

Nico shook his head again. "Hamish."

A finger of ice traced Javi's spine. He braced himself, lifted the bedspread, and looked under the bed. A rush of damp coldness swept over him like a thick fog, clinging to his skin and seeping into his pores. A familiar scent met his nose, but he couldn't place the aroma. He squinted, adjusting his eyes to the darkness.

The space under the bed was empty.

"SOMETHING IS VERY, very strange about this Hamish," Javi told Amparo the next morning over breakfast.

"Javi, I've told you a hundred times, imaginary friends are not unusual in children Nico's age. Especially under the circumstances."

"You do not understand. I do not believe this is an *imaginary* friend."

Amparo sighed and took her bowl to the sink. "You're right, I don't understand. If he's not imaginary, what is he?"

Javi bit his lip. How could he explain to her what he had seen, and make her believe? He barely believed it himself.

"I . . . I think Hamish is real."

"Real? If he's real, why haven't we seen him?"

Javi stared at his hands and said in a very soft voice, "I do not think we *can* see him."

"What do you mean, we can't see him? Either he's real

and we can see him or he's— Do you think Hamish is invisible?" Amparo looked at Javi.

Their eyes met for an instant, then he looked away.

"Oh, Javi, come now." Amparo pulled out the chair next to Javi and sat down. "You're not a five-year-old boy who believes in elves and goblins and people with superpowers. You're a bright eleven-year-old who knows that people can't make themselves invisible."

Javi felt his face grow hot. "I do—did—not say superpowers. I do not know *what* it is. I know only that it talk to Nico and teach him things and play with him. I see it!"

Amparo squeezed Javi's clenched fist. "Okay, calm down. I don't want us to argue about everything. It's just that what you're telling me is, well, it's just incredible. You can't expect me to believe—"

"I do not lie!"

"I didn't say you were lying." Amparo closed her eyes, taking a deep breath. "Okay, tell me what you saw."

"You do not believe me," Javi muttered.

"Tell me, and we'll try to figure out together what's happening."

Javi thought back to the previous night. "Last night, when I go upstairs, Nico is playing ball—he rolls it under the bed. Tití, the ball rolls back to him—*sola*—by itself. Nico say it is Hamish." He shivered at the memory.

"Maybe Fidel—"

"No, I look. There is nothing under the bed. ¡*Nada!* But when I lift the bedcover, I feel very cold, and I smell something sweet."

Javi glanced at his aunt. Her eyebrows puckered.

"See? You do not believe me," he said, looking back at his hands.

"That's not true. I believe you saw the ball rolling back to Nico. But I think there is a logical explanation, and I think I know what it is."

Javi looked up. "You do?"

"I'll bet the house has settled and the floor has a slant. In this area the soil is very spongy, and houses shift and settle constantly. Some homes can move as much as six or seven inches up and down on their piles"—one look at Javi's puzzled expression, and she went on to explain—" 'Piles' are the beams in the ground that support a house. I'll bet Nico was rolling the ball up a slight incline, and it naturally rolled back down to him."

Javi considered his aunt's explanation. "But how does—did—Nico learn to count?"

"We discussed that last night. He probably picked it up somewhere."

Javi shrugged. "Perhaps," he said.

But he was not convinced.

Later that morning Amparo went out to pick up some groceries, leaving Javi to baby-sit Nico. She gave Javi her cell-phone number just in case, with instructions to call her if they had any problems. She would be only a few minutes away by car.

While she was gone, Javi and Nico sat in the den, drawing. Nico was using his crayons to draw and color pictures in a large sketch pad Amparo had gotten him. Javi sat at Amparo's desk with his old sketch pad, sketching the footbridge and the oaks in the backyard.

He loved drawing. At his old school he had participated in a special art class for gifted students. His favorite subjects were gnarled, twisted trees and old wooden structures. He was using charcoal to make the scene appear more—what was the word Willo had used?—*ominous.*

Javi studied the oaks in the backyard with an artist's eye. Their branches reached out like the ancient, tortured claws of a giant bird. There was something angry in the twists and turns of those branches, something desperate in the way they reached outward, eternally begging, pleading, beckoning.

Somehow he understood their longing, their need. It was *his* longing, *his* need, *his* frustration and desperation to return to a life of safety and unity and love. Taking a piece of charcoal, he made bold, thick strokes that ended in spidery wisps. Then, going back and filling in the leaves, he rendered the oaks, rendered his emotions onto the stark white sheet.

He was so engrossed in what he was doing that it was several minutes before he noticed that a damp coldness had settled around him. He sniffed. There was that familiar sweet scent—the one from last night.

What was it?

It was getting stronger. Anise? Licorice?

"Nico, are you eating licorice?"

Nico looked up from his drawing. "No, but Hamish is."

"Hamish is here—in this room?"

"*Mm-hmm,* he's standing right beside you."

Javi jumped from his chair, yelling, *"Aaa-yiii!"* Tripping on his art bag, he fell to the floor. "Where . . . where is he now?"

Nico giggled as though Javi were performing a slapstick comedy act for his entertainment. "Javi *bobo!*"

"It's not funny, Nico," Javi said, his eyes scanning the room. "Where is he?"

"He's looking at your drawing."

Javi looked at the desk where his drawing lay. No one was near it. "I don't see Hamish, Nico. Do you see him?"

Nico nodded. "Hamish says your drawing is very scary. It looks like the evil thing in the woods."

"Evil thing? What evil thing?" Then the implication of what Nico said hit him. Javi felt the hair on the back of his neck rise. "Nico, how do you know what my drawing looks like? I haven't shown it to you, and you can't see it from where you're sitting."

"Hamish told me. He's looking at it."

Keeping his eyes on the area near the desk, Javi slid backward on the floor until he reached Nico's side. He took the little boy by the shoulders and turned Nico toward him, looking into his eyes.

"Listen to me carefully, Nico. What does Hamish look like?"

Nico held up his own sketch pad. On the page, a large sun peeked from one corner, smiling down on two little figures. Each figure had a circle for a head, a triangle for a body, and long, skinny rectangles for arms and legs—no fingers or feet, just arms and legs.

One of the figures had a brown smudge that looked like hair on top of its circle-head. Its triangular body and rectangular arms were red, and its rectangular legs were dark blue. Javi glanced at Nico: He was wearing blue jeans and a red shirt; his straight brown hair gleamed in the lamplight.

The other figure had yellow circular squiggles on its head. Its triangular body and rectangular arms were light blue; the rectangle-legs were pink.

Javi pointed at the second figure. "Who's this?"

Nico smiled. "Hamish. See? Gold, curly hair, like the *angelitos*."

"Like the little angels?" Goose bumps traveled up Javi's arms. Their grandmother's house was full of images of little blond angels. "But why . . . why isn't he wearing pants—is this a dress? Is Hamish a girl—an angel girl?"

Nico giggled. "Javi *bobo*. Hamish doesn't have wings—just blond angel *rizos*. He's wearing shorts, see? And he wears long white socks, up to his knees. And this is his shirt." Nico pointed to the blue triangle. "It's one of those shirts like the *marineros* wear, see?"

"Like sailors wear?"

Nico nodded. "Like the sailors in San Juan. When Mami and Papi took us on the big boat for a tour."

Javi winced at the mention of his parents. He remembered that day—they had toured one of the naval ships that had docked for a week. He remembered the clear blue sky, the smell of the sea air, Mami's laughter when Papi told a silly joke.

Javi bolted upright. The details in Nico's description of Hamish—the blond angel curls, the white kneesocks, the sailor suit. It was almost as if Hamish were a real person.

How could a five-year-old come up with such vivid details?

Unless . . .

JAVI DROPPED THE SKETCH PAD and spun to look at the area near his desk. Still he could see nothing unusual.

"Nico," he whispered, "is Hamish still looking at my drawing?"

"Um-hmm," Nico replied, smiling and nodding.

"Tell . . . tell him to leave."

"Leave?" he squeaked.

"Yes, leave. Tell him to leave *now*."

Nico grabbed Javi's arm. His beaming face had crumpled into a worried frown.

"Noooo!" he wailed, shaking his head. "Please don't make Hamish go."

"I don't want him in this house anymore. I don't want him near you . . . near us."

"But where will he go?" Nico's voice quivered.

"Back. Back where he came from. Back where he was before we arrived."

"But he can't. He's afraid."

Javi stiffened. "Afraid? What does . . . *he* have to be afraid of?"

"The evil one. The man. Out there." Nico pointed toward the footbridge.

A piece of ice dropped into Javi's stomach. His skin turned to gooseflesh. "Something is out there? Something worse than what's in here?" Images from his nightmare returned. He remembered Willo's words: *Something wicked's in those woods.*

"Please, Javi." Nico squeezed Javi's arm. His eyes, brimming with tears, pleaded. "Please don't make Hamish go. He's little, like me. Here he's safe. The evil one can't come inside."

Javi shook himself free of Nico's grasp. He hated to see Nico cry after he'd been so happy again, but he had to remain firm. Nico was only a baby. He didn't know who or *what* Hamish was. Neither did Javi, but his gut told him Hamish was dangerous.

"No," Javi said. "No, he can't stay here. He doesn't have to go to the woods. Tell him—tell him to go home."

"He can't go home. He doesn't have a home anymore. He's looked and looked, but it's gone."

"Where are his"—Javi couldn't believe what he was going to say—"his parents? Can't he go to his parents?"

"He's tried. He can't find them. He doesn't know where they've gone."

Javi clenched his jaw. "Well, that's too bad. He can't stay here. Will he go if you ask him to?"

Nico gazed into his brother's eyes. He nodded. Tears streamed down his cheeks.

"Then tell him to go. Now."

Nico's lower lip trembled. His face puckered. "No."

"What do you mean, no? I'm your big brother. I'm the one responsible for us now that Mami and Papi are gone, and I'm telling you he has to go!"

Nico's jaw jutted out. He stamped his foot. "No! No! *No!*"

Javi's eyes flashed. "Don't you disobey me, Nico. Tell—!"

Suddenly Javi was covered in a dank, cold sweat. It clung to his skin; it iced his bones. The smell of anise was overpowering, nauseating.

Javi's heart slammed against his chest. He grabbed Nico and ran to the opposite wall. "Get away from us! Stay! Stay away! Nico, tell him to leave. *Now!*"

"*No!*" Nico screamed, struggling to free himself from Javi's grasp. "*No, no, no!*"

"Hey, hey, hey! What's going on here?" Amparo ran in, still carrying two bags of groceries. When she saw Javi, pale faced and grasping a struggling, squirming Nico, she dropped the bags.

Nico ripped away from Javi and ran to his aunt's open arms, screaming and crying.

"*Dios mío,* Javier, what is happening here?" She held the sobbing child against her chest. "*Shh-hh, shh-hh,* Nico. It's okay, everything's going to be all right."

Javi just stared at her, jaw clenched and hands squeezed into tight fists.

"He—he wants me to make Hamish go away," Nico sobbed.

Amparo looked at Javi as if she couldn't believe what she was hearing. "Javier, how could you? Are you trying to traumatize this child further?" She spoke to Javi in English, but switched back to Spanish for Nico. "*Shh-hh,* Nico, it's okay. Hamish doesn't have to go. Hamish can stay. *Shh-hh . . .*"

"No!" Javi yelled. "He cannot stay! You do not understand! You do not—!"

"That's enough, Javi! Go to your room. You've done enough damage. I'll be up later to speak to you."

Javi pressed himself against the wall. In Spanish, he yelled, "I'm not going anywhere until Nico makes that . . . *thing* go away!"

"Javier, I said go to your room!"

"No! I don't want him here. He can't stay! He's—"

A loud rumbling drowned out Javi's words. The walls and floor began to shake. Objects on the shelves and pictures on the walls rattled and shimmied. The wooden desk chair wobble-walked across the room. Books tumbled from the shelves, crashing to the floor.

"Hurry, Nico, Javi," Amparo said, lifting Nico. "Come stand under the door frame. It's the safest place."

Before Javi could move or Amparo could reach the door, it slammed shut, and they were wrapped in silence.

Amparo and Nico clung to each other. Javi remained plastered against the wall, his heart thundering in his ears.

In the silence Nico let out a tiny sob and buried his head deeper into Amparo's chest. She rocked him in her arms, making soft cooing sounds, trying to calm him.

"It's okay, just another earthquake, that's all. A big one this time. But it's over now, it's all over."

"Javi, I'd like to speak to you," Amparo said, poking her head inside Javi's room.

After a tense lunch during which no one spoke, Javi had gone upstairs to read. Now he laid the book on his stomach and stared at the ceiling.

"Please climb down here where I can see you."

"I can hear you up here," he mumbled.

"But I can't see you. Please . . . we need to talk."

Javi heaved a gusty sigh and climbed down from his bunk. He sat on Nico's bed, staring at his Nikes.

Amparo pulled up a chair and sat facing him. "What happened this morning? Why did you make Nico cry?"

He began to jiggle his leg, making the bed shake. Amparo placed a calming hand on his knee. His leg relaxed.

"Javi?"

"I am sorry I make Nico cry. I do not want him to be sad."

"Then why?"

Javi began to nibble his thumbnail. He bit it to the quick and kept biting.

Amparo took his hand and pulled it away from his face. She held it in her warm, soft hand. "I'm listening."

"You do—will—not believe me," he muttered, refusing to look at her face.

"I believed you before."

"Not completely. You said there is a . . . logical explanation."

"And wasn't there?"

Javi's shoulders stiffened; he pulled his hand from hers. "I do not think so."

"Well, try me again."

"*Bien,* you want to know so very bad, I tell you." This time Javi looked up at her, glaring defiantly. "But I know you will not believe me."

Javi went on to tell his aunt about how he and Nico had been drawing in the den. He described his landscape and how he was lost in his drawing when a damp coldness enveloped him. Then he told her about the licorice smell and how Nico said Hamish had been eating licorice and was standing beside him, looking at his drawing.

"And, Tití, Nico says my drawing is scary, and he knows I draw the trees outside. But he is across the room. He cannot know what I draw . . . unless someone—someone who looks over my shoulder—tells him."

Javi glanced up at his aunt. Her face was calm, blank; he could not tell what she was thinking. He ventured further.

"But there is no one in the room with us—no one standing by the desk— *¡Nadie!* Then Nico shows me a picture he draw of Hamish. It is a little boy with yellow *rizos*—curls. I feel"—Javi looked at his bitten thumbnail—"I feel fear. I do not want Hamish in this house. I grow angry with Nico because he does not tell him to leave."

Amparo exhaled slowly, as if she had been holding her breath. "I see. Well . . . there must be—"

"A logical explanation?" Javi shook his head. "You mean like this?"

He stood and picked up Nico's ball from the corner of the room. "You say the floor is crooked?"

Amparo nodded. "Tilted, maybe, down away from your bed. So when you put the ball on the floor, it should roll away from the bed, toward the shelves behind us."

"You are correct. It is tilted. But look." Javi placed the ball on the floor, where Nico had been sitting. He held it with one finger, steadying it, then let go. The ball began to roll.

It rolled under the bed and stayed there.

JAVI SPENT THE NEXT MORNING helping Amparo dust the house. While Amparo dusted and vacuumed the upstairs, Javi dusted the downstairs rooms. At the same time he kept an eye on Nico, who was playing with Fidel.

As Javi dusted the mantel over the fireplace, he tried to push aside the resentment that part of his summer vacation had to be taken up with doing chores. Mami had never made him do housework. And even Papi took care of the yard himself or hired a man to help.

Nico's giggles returned Javi's thoughts to the present. He turned to see what could be so funny. Fidel was running back and forth on the carpet as though he were chasing something. ZsaZsa and Misifú were curled together on the couch, watching with disinterest, their eyelids half lowered in boredom. Nico fell back on his heels, laughing at the fool dog who was chasing and pouncing, chasing and pouncing.

Javi chuckled and wagged his head, turning to the mantel to resume his dusting. On the mantel sat a wooden picture frame that held an old photograph of Amparo and her older brother—Javi's father—hugging, heads together, and smiling into the camera. As Javi reached to pick it up, a movement in the mirror above the mantel caught his eye.

He looked up and froze, his mouth gaping.

The mirror showed the scene behind him: The cats curled on the couch. Nico sitting back on his heels, laughing. And Fidel chasing and pouncing on a little blond boy dressed in a pale blue sailor suit with short pants and white kneesocks. The little boy appeared to be laughing (though Javi could not hear him), and whenever Fidel pounced, the boy would get up, run a short distance, squat, and let Fidel pounce on him once more. Each time Fidel pounced on the boy, he fell right through him, landing on the floor.

Javi spun around.

The little boy was gone, but Fidel continued to run and pounce, run and pounce.

"*¡Ayiiiii!*" yelled Javi. "*¡Lo ví, lo ví! ¡Tití, lo ví!*"

Javi ran to Nico, grabbed his arm, and pulled him toward the hall. "Tití, Tití!" he screamed. "Where is he, Nico? Where's Hamish?"

With all the commotion, Fidel forgot about his chasing game and ran to Javi's side, jumping and barking as though he were asking what all the yelling was about.

"Are you going to make him leave?" Nico whined.

"No, just tell me where he is."

Nico pointed to where Javi had seen Hamish playing with Fidel. "He's sitting on the floor."

"Don't let him go anywhere, understand? Tití! Hurry, come down here!"

Amparo clumped down the stairs, a kerchief over her brown curls. Her face wore the expression of one who's looking for the fire.

"What is it?" she cried. "Are you all right?"

"*¡Lo ví, lo ví! ¡Tití, lo ví!*" Javi pointed toward the middle of the room.

"What did you see? What's wrong?"

"I see him! I see Hamish!"

Amparo stared at her nephew. Her jaw dropped.

Javi could tell she didn't believe him. "No, it is true. I see him in the mirror—when I dust."

"In the mirror?"

"Yes, come here." Javi took his aunt's arm and tugged her to where he had been standing. "I look in the mirror—here—and I see—I saw—Fidel chasing Hamish."

Amparo looked in the mirror. Her gaze slid back to Javi. "I don't see anything."

"But you must, he is—" When Javi looked in the mirror, toward the spot on the floor, he saw nothing but empty carpet. "Where is he, Nico? Where is Hamish?"

"He got scared. He's hiding."

"Nooo! I told you not to let him leave!"

Nico's lower lip began to tremble. "But—but—"

"It's okay, Nico," Amparo told him softly. "Javier, let it go. Don't upset Nico again."

"But it is proof—I have—I had—proof—"

"Proof of what?"

"That Hamish is real. And more." Javi grabbed his aunt's arm and squeezed, desperate to make her understand.

"Okay, Javi, let go. You're hurting me." Amparo pried Javi's fingers from her arm and rubbed the aching spot. "I'm trying to believe you, Javi. But this is so—"

Javi's eyes pleaded with her. "You must believe me. I know what he is now."

"What he is? What do you mean?"

"When Fidel chase him, and he catch him, Fidel jump on Hamish. And when he jump . . . he go right through him—*como aire*, like air."

Amparo frowned. "What are you saying, Javi?"

"I think—I think Hamish is *un espíritu*—a spirit."

15

"JAVI, JAVI, WHAT AM I going to do with you?"

Amparo sank onto the nearest chair. Her face was pale. She looked tired.

"I've tried to listen to your theories. I've tried to explain about Nico's need to create Hamish. But you insist on making something more of the situation. And now this." She placed her hands on her knees, rubbing them as if they hurt. "I simply don't know what to say. A ghost? You expect me to believe that we are being haunted by a little boy's ghost?"

Javi knelt beside her and took her hand in his. "*Sí*, Tití, haunted. That is it. Do you not see how it make sense?"

Amparo gave his hand a tiny squeeze and stroked his cheek, gazing sadly into his eyes. "No, *m'ijo*, I do not see. I don't believe in ghosts or spirits or hauntings. I believe in other things, tangible things—rational explanations for the tricks the mind can play on a person. That is my career, my life—to understand the human mind."

Javi stiffened and pulled away. "You think this is in my mind? Do you not believe I see him?"

"I believe you saw *something*. But—"

"But you think I am *loco*?"

"No, *m'ijo*, of course I don't think you're crazy. But you've gone through a lot this past month. A great deal of grief and frustration—all very stressful. These emotions can sometimes play tricks with a person's mind. Cause you to imagine—"

"Now you think I imagine—the way Nico imagines? I tell you I do not imagine! I saw him! How can you explain that the boy I saw look like the boy Nico draw—the boy Nico *describe*?"

"Maybe Nico's drawing and his description influenced what you saw."

Javi said nothing, but he hoped the scowl on his face told her how he felt.

Amparo sighed. "Javi, listen to me. I've spent my whole adult life studying how to explain the tricks that the mind plays on people. You can't expect me to simply accept this . . . this phenomenon you say exists in my house without first trying to find a rational explanation. Something scientific."

Javi stood, balling up his hands. "There is no scientific explanation for the smell and the cold I feel when he is near. No explanation for the ball that rolls up the hill instead of down, or for how Nico seems to know things that only someone else can tell him."

"Maybe not on the surface, but if you're patient, Javi, we may be able to find an answer. Together."

"When? When Hamish harms Nico? Or one of us?"

"We have no reason to believe—"

"*You* have no reason to believe!" The veins along Javi's temples pulsed. Rage against the injustice of not being believed churned inside him. "*You* do not trust in me!"

"Javi, please try to see this from my point of view. I have lived in this house for ten years. If it were haunted, don't you think I would have noticed something unusual?"

Javi bit his lips together and glared at her, refusing to answer.

Amparo tried again. "Aren't ghosts supposed to make odd things happen? Doors opening and closing by themselves, objects moving or falling on their own? I've never seen that happen."

At that moment the picture frame on the mantel—the one with the photo of Amparo and Javi's father—toppled over and fell with a crash onto the hearth. The glass shattered into a thousand pieces.

Amparo and Javi stared at the fallen picture and shattered glass. Slowly Javi turned his gaze toward Amparo. Her hands had flown to her chest; she sat upright in the chair. When their eyes met, his narrowed into tiny slits and his mouth twisted.

"Explain *that* with science!" he yelled, and ran from the room.

"Javi?" Amparo stepped onto the deck. "Is this yours?"

Javi looked up from his chair, where he had been spending the afternoon sketching. Amparo was holding a book. He leaned in closer to get a better look. It was a book of ghost stories.

"Yes, that is a book that I select at the library. Willo get—got—it for me."

Amparo pulled up a patio chair and sat facing him. "Javi, I am very pleased that you are checking out books from the library. Reading books you like will help you learn English more quickly. And I don't wish to discourage you from choosing your own books . . ." Amparo paused.

"But?"

"Well, I am a bit concerned. This book is about ghosts, and—"

"It is a book of *stories* about ghosts."

"Yes, stories about ghosts, which I wouldn't normally mind—I know how much fun it can be to read scary stories—but what concerns me is that soon after you checked out a book of ghost stories, you claimed to see a ghost."

Javi's mouth dropped open. So that was it. That's why she had his book with her.

"But—but, Tití, I did not yet read the book!"

"I see . . . well, perhaps seeing the book at the library and bringing it home placed a suggestion in your subconscious, causing—"

"What! I do not understand what you say. Do you speak to me as if I am a patient? Do you think you are my"—Javi tried to remember the word Willo had used when they first met—"shrink?"

"No, Javi, of course not. I just mean—"

"You just mean that you do not believe that I see a real ghost—that *Hamish* is a real ghost—and now you try to prove that I make it up."

Amparo sighed. "Javi, I'm just trying to understand. Perhaps seeing the book, even if you hadn't read any of the stories yet, caused you to imagine—"

"Again you say I imagine—like little Nico. *I* do *not* imagine. And *Nico* does not imagine. *You* are the one who imagine. You are the one who need to believe that there is no ghost—that the ghost is in our heads!"

"Javi, calm down and stop screaming. I will not allow you to speak to me this way. I am your aunt, your guardian. I deserve more respect than this. You may not continue to be so disrespectful."

"Disrespectful? And what do you call it when you go into my room and search?"

"I have not been searching your room. I—"

"Not been searching my room? Then how do you find this?" Javi ripped the book from her hands. Amparo flinched. "I put this in my room. To find it, you must go into Nico's and my room."

Amparo drew herself up to her full height. "I will take no more disrespect from you, Javier. I did find the book in your room. But I was not searching—I was vacuuming. Anyway, this is my house, and I am the adult here. I have a right to enter any room I want."

"You say it is *our* room. You say—"

"Javier, not one more word from you. I am your guardian, and I set the rules. Your room is your room, that is true. And I will allow you as much privacy as any child deserves. But you are a child, and sometimes I must enter your room, even—"

"But—"

Amparo held up one finger and cocked an eyebrow. Javi swallowed his words of protest. He clenched his fists and bit his lower lip.

"Yes, even when you and Nico are not in the room. And since you seem so fond of your room, you will spend the rest of the day there. I will bring you your dinner, and you will eat alone. Perhaps that will give you some time to reflect on your attitude. I know your parents taught you respect. Think about that."

Amparo reached over and slid Javi's book from his lap. He started to snatch it back, but Amparo again cocked an eyebrow. She gave him a penetrating stare. He looked away, clenching his fists again.

"For the time being," his aunt said, "I don't want you reading ghost stories, or anything to do with ghosts. I also don't want to discuss ghosts or hauntings or any other supernatural phenomena. Do you understand?"

Javi just stared at the wooden deck. His fists clenched and unclenched. He bit his lip so hard he drew blood.

A quick and severe shake that rattled the windows made Javi jump from his chair. His sketch pad fell to his feet. Behind her, Amparo's chair flipped over and slid off the deck, landing in her favorite flower bed.

"*Bien*, I go to my room." Javi glowered at his aunt, his heart thumping. "But where I really want to be is back home—in Puerto Rico—and away from this land of shakes and quakes!"

Tired of lying on the bed listening to music, and still fuming over the indignity of being treated like a baby and sent to his room, Javi searched for something to do.

Maybe he could read.

But the thought just reminded him of how Tití Amparo had taken away his book of ghost stories. She was right about one thing, reading scary stories *was* fun. It might have been a tolerable way to pass his hours of solitary confinement.

Then he remembered the other book Willo had checked out for him—the one about unsolved mysteries. Mystery was at least as interesting a topic as ghosts.

Where had he put it?

Javi rummaged around the cluttered room; then he remembered where he'd last seen the book. He had been lying on the floor near the bed, paging through it, when Amparo had called him for dinner last night. Maybe Nico had kicked it under the bed.

Javi lifted the edge of the bedspread and peeked under the bed. Sure enough, the book lay open near the far wall. No wonder Amparo hadn't seen it. If she had, she'd probably have confiscated it along with the ghost stories.

Feeling rebellious, but also knowing that Amparo had not directly prohibited the reading of mystery stories, Javi reached under the bed and pulled the book toward him. The moment he looked at the open pages, he froze.

The pages displayed several old black-and-white photographs. One of the pictures made Javi's stomach feel as if he'd just gone down the steepest crest of a roller coaster. Although blurry, it showed a little curly-haired blond boy wearing a light-colored sailor suit with white kneesocks, and sitting on a tall, expensive-looking rocking horse.

Javi's heart smacked his rib cage. "This is him! This is the boy in the mirror!"

16

"THIS HAD BETTER BE GOOD," Willo said the next morning, as she walked into Javi's room. Her hair was windblown, and her face was flushed. "I try never to be up before ten during summer vacation."

"Yes, this is very good." Javi set his earphones aside and sat up, swinging his legs over the side of the bunk. "I believe that Nico's new friend—"

"His imaginary friend?"

"Yes, yes, his imaginary friend—he is not truly imaginary."

Willo took a step toward Javi. "Not imaginary—then what is he?"

"That is what Tití say. Yesterday, when I tell her, we argue—we argue too much—that is when she punish me and send me to my room."

Willo snorted. "You were grounded? In your first week here?"

"I am what?"

"Grounded—punished."

Javi nodded. "Yes, grounded. Yesterday I may not leave my room for the rest of the day. And I was very bumped about it."

Willo giggled. "You were what?"

"It is a new expression I learn on television—bumped. It is not correct?"

Willo thought for a moment. "Oh, bummed! It's pronounced *'bummmmed,'* just an *m*, no *p*. *Bummmmed.*"

"*Bummmmed.* Yes, that is it."

"Everyone gets bummed when they're grounded. It's no fun. So what did you do? Amparo's usually pretty easygoing."

"I tell Tití that Hamish is a ghost."

"You what?" Willo's eyes glistened like emeralds under a spotlight. She was wearing a kelly-green jacket, and her eyes had picked up the color.

"I tell her Hamish is a ghost."

"Cripes! Are you sure? How did you find out?"

Willo sat on Nico's bed, listening intently to Javi's story as he told her about the strange occurrences he had witnessed over the past few days. He told her about the ball rolling uphill from under the bed. He also told her how Nico seemed to be learning English, although neither Javi nor his aunt had taught him the words he'd learned. Then Javi told her about the scene in the den when he and Nico were drawing. He showed her the picture that Nico had drawn of Hamish and told her how Nico had described the clothes he had tried to draw on the little stick figure.

Finally, Javi told her about the boy he saw in the mirror—the boy who looked just like Nico had described

Hamish—and how when Fidel pounced on the boy, he fell right through him.

"Then, when I tell Tití, we argue. She say I imagine because I read a book of ghost stories. She take away the book, then she send me to my room. That is when I find"— Javi reached under his mattress and pulled out a book— "this."

Willo eyed the book. "That's the library book."

"Yes, *Unsolved Mysteries of the Twentieth Century.* And you cannot guess what I find inside."

"What? What, I'm dying here—tell me." Willo bounced on the bed.

"You remember the name of Nico's imaginary friend?"

"Nico's friend? Sure, Hamish. We've just been talking about him—the ghost, *duh-uh.*"

"I mean the complete name. You remember?"

"Well, I think so. Isn't it Hamish Brenden McTavish?"

"Yes, it is. And do you not think that is a too unusual name?"

"'*Very* unusual.' Sure, I guess."

"That is what I say to Tití Amparo. I always say, 'How can Nico know such a name?' "

"Okay, you've got me. How?"

"I believe I know how. Look at this." Javi opened the book to a spot marked with a torn piece of paper.

He pointed to the chapter title: "The Unsolved Kidnapping of Hamish Brenden McTavish."

17

WILLO LOOKED UP AT JAVI. She looked down at the book. She swallowed. "This is about Hamish? Nico's Hamish?"

Javi nodded. "I believe so . . . Here, read—in voice tall—read."

" 'In voice tall'?"

"It is 'voice high'? *En voz alta*. Read not in your head. Read to me."

"Okay, out loud, okay." Willo took the book and began to read:

Hamish Brenden McTavish, age six, was the only child of wealthy San Francisco businessman Brenden Shamus McTavish and his wife, Lorna, who had a vacation home in the Orinda hills. On the night of December 30, 1932, during the depths of the Great Depression, the McTavishes' son was abducted from the Orinda home. A ransom note was the only clue left behind—on little Hamish's bed. The McTavishes were instructed to gather money together and await further orders.

The day after the kidnapping, northern California was hit by a terrible storm. High winds, incessant rainfall, and floods ravaged the countryside. In the Oakland and Orinda hills, the constant rain eroded the earth, causing landslides and weakening tree roots. An old, tall pine near the McTavish vacation home toppled over during the storm, crushing the roof of the house and almost trapping Mr. and Mrs. McTavish.

With their vacation home destroyed, the McTavishes were forced to leave the house before their son was found. They took lodging in a nearby hotel, and Mr. McTavish returned daily to the house, searching for new instructions from the kidnapper. At the front door, he regularly left a fresh bag of licorice drops, Hamish's favorite candy, in case Hamish returned on his own. But neither Hamish nor further instructions ever appeared.

Javi interrupted the story. "You see? You think . . . perhaps . . . the wicked thing in the woods—the thing Hamish fears—is the kidnapper?"

Willo glanced up. "That's what I was thinking. It must be the kidnapper's ghost. No wonder the poor little boy is terrified of him."

"He is not a boy. He is a ghost also." Javi resisted a shudder, but his skin grew goose bumps. "Hamish even smell of the licorice drops he likes to eat."

Willo made a face and continued to read:

The police searched the entire area, questioned possible suspects, and tried to follow up various clues.

After several months the few leads the police had grew cold. They began to suspect that if the kidnapper had been hiding with Hamish in or near the Orinda woods, they may both have perished in the storm.

Two months after the kidnapping, the McTavishes returned to their San Francisco home. Despite a large reward that Mr. McTavish offered for any information on the whereabouts of his son or the kidnapper, no one ever came forward. To this day the kidnapping remains unsolved.

When Willo was done, Javi took back the book and flipped though some pages. "Look," he said, "these are the pictures. The pictures of Hamish."

Javi pointed out the photo of Hamish on the rocking horse—the photo that showed every detail that Nico had described. The notation beneath the photo indicated the picture had been taken at Christmas, one week before the little boy's kidnapping.

"Crocs on a rock!" Willo said after taking her time studying the photographs of Hamish. She pulled her feet onto the bed and hugged her legs, resting her chin on her knees. Her eyes shone.

"The real live ghost of Hamish Brenden McTavish is haunting your aunt's house. Crackers!"

"You—you believe me?"

"Well, of course I believe you. It's right here in the book, isn't it? I always sort of thought something strange was going on. Anyway, there are too many similarities between your story and Hamish's story for this not to be true."

Javi nodded, relieved someone finally believed him.

"Little Hamish disappeared, and probably died, somewhere in those woods." Willo gazed out the window and shivered. "So what will you do now? Tell Amparo?"

"I cannot! She forbids me to speak of ghosts or to read any books about ghosts. I wish too much to tell her and to show her this book, but she will only say that I read the book first, then made up a story about how I saw Hamish in the mirror."

"*Hmm,* you're probably right. Too bad she found that ghost book first."

"Yes, very too bad. Also, I think Tití does not *wish* to believe this house is haunted and that Hamish is a ghost." Javi sighed. "She says there must be a logical, scientific explanation for these things."

"Well, in a way, she's right," Willo said, scooting back on the bed and leaning against the wall. "Parapsychology is a legitimate science, but because it deals with supernatural phenomena, it's having difficulty gaining the recognition it deserves. Some of the most respected universities in the world have departments of parapsychology."

Javi's mouth gaped. He stared at Willo as though she had been speaking Chinese. "Para-what? I not—I *do* not understand."

"Oh, sorry." Willo grinned sheepishly. "Sometimes I go on and forget that other kids don't read the same things I do."

"Please repeat, but use small words. There is a science . . . ?"

"Yes, parapsychology is the study of paranormal or supernatural occurrences, like ghosts and extrasensory perception and psychokinesis and clairvoyance—"

"Stop! Small words."

"Right. ESP, or extrasensory perception, means communicating or sensing by means other than the usual physical senses, like touch, hearing, seeing. Take clairvoyance. That's when you know something is happening or going to happen without seeing it with your eyes or having someone tell you. Haven't you ever just known something was going to happen—maybe something really bad—and then it did?"

The hair on Javi's arms stood on end. His stomach felt queasy. The room spun.

"Javi? Are you okay? You look like you're going to throw up. Here, lean over and put your head between your knees. Take slow, deep breaths . . . That better?"

He did as she instructed. He breathed deeply, slowly. He nodded.

"What happened?" Willo asked.

Javi sat up. "The night before my parents died . . . I have a *pesadilla*, a bad dream—"

"A nightmare?"

"Yes, a nightmare. I dream they are killed in a car accident. I tell them, but they say, 'Do not worry, it is only a *pesadilla*.' But it does not feel like one. It feels very real."

"Is that what happened? Did they die in a car crash?"

Javi nodded, wiping away tears. "Why did they not listen to me? Why did I not make them listen? It is my fault they are dead. I must make them listen!"

Willo placed her arm around his shoulders. "No, Javi, don't blame yourself. After Mom died, I used to tell myself that if I had done this or if I had done that, she wouldn't have gotten sick. It rips you up inside, but it doesn't help. Sometimes I still wonder if there wasn't some magic I could have performed, something . . . That's what got me interested in reading about parapsychology."

Javi gave Willo a watery smile. Willo blushed and re-moved her arm from his shoulders. She scooted away, plac-ing her hands awkwardly on her lap.

They sat silently, thinking. Javi hadn't told Amparo about his nightmare. He hadn't told anyone but his parents. It occurred to him that if his parents hadn't taken his nightmare seriously, they might not have believed that Amparo's house was haunted, either. Maybe it wasn't Am-paro's fault that she couldn't believe. Maybe all grown-ups had trouble believing in such things.

"Javi," Willo said, breaking into his thoughts, "if we could get Amparo to look at this from a scientific point of view—"

"I tell you, I do not think she *wants* to believe. We had very big arguments yesterday about ghosts. That is why I was what you call grounded. And the day I screamed at Nico to make Hamish go away, I think she did not ground me because the earthquake frightened us too much."

"Earthquake?"

"Yes, very, very big. Much bigger than the one yester-day. Even Tití said it was a very big one. You did not feel?"

Willo frowned. "I didn't feel a thing. Yesterday, either. And what's even more strange is that I didn't hear anything about them on the six o'clock news. News shows love to re-port earthquakes. Even tiny ones."

18

"WHERE HAVE YOU BEEN?" Amparo called from the kitchen. "I was starting to get worried."

Javi had just taken Fidel for a long walk through the neighborhood. After an hour he had reluctantly returned to the house. He was not anxious to feel or smell or hear about Hamish again. But he didn't want to leave Nico alone with him for too long, either. When he entered the kitchen, Javi was met with the spicy aroma of freshly made spaghetti sauce.

"Fidel was having a good walk. I did not want to stop him."

"Oh, Fidel, *huh*?" She didn't sound convinced.

"You do not believe that, either?"

Amparo looked as if she were going to say something but stopped herself. She grabbed a white napkin and dangled it in front of her. "Truce, okay? Let's not start another argument. Let's try to have a pleasant dinner."

Javi shrugged. He unleashed Fidel and placed the leash on its hook. The little black Scottie padded off to the living room to join the cats.

"Javi, please call Nico to dinner. The pasta is already overcooked."

Javi looked at her as if to say, *So that's my fault, too?* but looked away when he saw the hurt expression in his aunt's eyes.

He left the kitchen without saying another word and found Nico in the living room watching *Sesame Street.* ZsaZsa was curled on his lap, and Misifú was draped behind him on the back of the couch. Her fluffy tail hung over his shoulder and twitched periodically.

"Dinner, Nico. Turn off the TV."

Nico pressed the OFF button and pushed ZsaZsa from his lap. She gave him an indignant glare, jerking her tail at him. He leaned down and gave her an apologetic kiss on the head.

Javi grinned. "Hungry?"

"*Mm-hmm.* So is Hamish."

Javi's grin froze. He clenched his fists. "Hamish can't eat with us anymore. Tell him to stay here. You can play with him after dinner."

He grabbed Nico's arm and pulled him toward the kitchen, anxious to get away from Hamish.

As usual, Nico sat across from Javi and Amparo sat between them at the head of the table. Amparo had picked up some salad dressings she thought the boys might like, and she set the bottles of dressing on the table beside the big bowl of salad greens. Next to the salad she set a large covered platter, a covered bowl, and a plate of garlic bread.

The garlic smelled wonderful, and Javi realized he was

starving. He filled his salad plate with tiny red and
green and yellow leaves of different shapes. He covered
the greens in dressing and turned to see how Nico was
doing.

Facing his plate, as if he were eating, Nico was slowly
scooting the chair next to him away from the table. He
stopped for a moment and looked up, meeting Javi's gaze.
His face took on an expression Javi had seen many times
when he had caught Nico playing with Javi's best colored
pencils—pencils Nico had been specifically told not to
touch. Quickly Nico's expression slid from guilt to sheer
innocence.

"What are you doing, Nico?"

He smiled. "I love you, Javi."

"Oh no, you're not getting out of this so easily."

"Javi," said Amparo, "what's gotten into you? Nico just
told you he loved you. Why are you scolding him?"

Javi glared at Nico. "He knows why."

"Well, I don't. Enlighten me."

"What?"

"Fill me in—tell me what Nico has done."

"Tití, you will not understand."

"Try me."

Javi looked down at his plate. "I do not wish to talk
about it."

"Then let's not hear anything more about it. That
means, let Nico eat in peace."

Trying to resign himself to the situation, Javi finished
his salad and began to serve himself some pasta. When he
uncovered the large platter, he stopped.

"Why is the spaghetti not mixed with the *salsa?*"

Amparo set down her fork. "Not mixed with the sauce?

Is that how you're used to eating it—all mixed up with the sauce?"

Javi nodded. "Mami always make—made—a meat *salsa*—sauce. And she mixed them and served them in a big bowl."

"Oh, well, this is the Italian way of doing it. You serve the spaghetti, then spoon some sauce on top. Like this." Amparo took Nico's plate and began to serve the pasta. "And the sauce is meatless today. Sometimes we can try it your way, sometimes this way. How's that? Then we won't get tired of the same spaghetti dish every time. It's nice to have a change once in a while."

Javi sighed. Change. In the past month, his life had been nothing but change. He would have given anything to make things go back to the way they were.

He watched his aunt serve Nico the spaghetti and spoon some sauce on top. He did the same. He tasted his spaghetti. It was redder and tangier than his mother's, but surprisingly good. Maybe there were some things Amparo could cook well.

He was about to tell her so when he looked across the table at Nico. His brother had placed a little spaghetti and sauce on his salad plate and was scooting it in front of the empty chair with his elbow. All the while, he was slurping spaghetti noodles as though nothing unusual was happening.

Javi's eyes narrowed. Nico glanced at him and froze. Then he took another forkful of noodles and stared up at the ceiling, slurping spaghetti.

Javi tried to eat, but his appetite was gone. He could not bear to eat at the same table with that . . . that thing. Even the fact that it was the ghost of a small, cute child didn't make the idea of Hamish any easier to bear.

Acid began to churn in his stomach. His palms grew cold and sweaty. He wanted so badly to scream at Nico to get rid of Hamish, he thought he'd burst.

Finally he couldn't hold it in any longer. He snuck a peek at his aunt. Amparo was absorbed in her food, apparently relishing the salad.

"Nico," he whispered, so his aunt wouldn't hear. "Nico!"

His little brother continued to stare at the ceiling, seemingly oblivious to Javi's urgent whispering. Javi narrowed his eyes, staring at Nico, willing Nico to look at him.

Nico brought his gaze down to his plate and stuffed another clump of long noodles into his mouth, slurping noisily. Then he turned away from Javi and resumed his inspection of the ceiling.

Javi knew Nico was ignoring him, and this knowledge only made his stomach churn more violently. Glancing quickly at Amparo, he reached under the table with his foot and gave Nico a soft kick. Startled, Nico jerked to attention, turning toward Javi.

Nico's spaghetti-splattered cheeks and large cow eyes did little to soften Javi's mood. He glowered at Nico, telling him with his eyes to get rid of Hamish. Nico returned the stare with a look of defiance, pursed his lips, and set his chin in that stubborn way Javi knew so well.

This would not be easy. Now that Nico had dug in his heels, there was no way a mere staring match was going to change his mind.

"I told you not to bring him to the table!" Javi whispered, his eyes flashing. "Tell him to go. Anywhere—I don't care where. But he can't stay at the table!"

Amparo looked up. "What's going on here?"

Javi and Nico continued their staring match, ignoring Amparo.

"Have you finished eating, Javier?"

Javier. She was back to using his full name. As if that could intimidate him.

"I am no longer hungry," he said without taking his gaze from Nico.

"Then perhaps you should go to your room and let Nico eat. It's my night to wash dishes, anyway." Amparo rose and stepped to the refrigerator.

Javi's gaze slid to the empty chair. His upper lip curled with distaste. It was all *his* fault. Hamish's. He had even turned Javi's baby brother against him. As he stared at the chair, he felt his stomach rumble and roll. He squeezed his fists until the knuckles turned white.

"Javier?" Amparo clinked a few bottles in the fridge. "Did you hear me?"

Without a word, Javi rose, sliding his chair away with the back of his legs. A hot flash, like a bolt of lightning, rushed through him. He glared at the empty chair through narrowed slits.

This is your fault! his mind screamed. *You can't even let us eat in peace. Go away! Leave us alone!*

The empty chair wobbled, then rock-rock-rocked from side to side. With incredible speed, the chair skated backward across the wooden floor, slammed into the wall, and flung forward from the impact. It lay there, legs in the air, motionless.

On the table, at the empty spot the chair had left, Nico's salad plate began to rattle. Nico reached out to stop it from falling. Before he could touch it, the plate spun off the table and flew like a Frisbee across the room, crashing into the wall.

The plate instantly shattered, showering the chair and the floor with bits of china that pinged like hail. It left the wall covered with spaghetti noodles, bits of salad greens, and red sauce that dripped toward the floor like streaks of blood.

19

AS AMPARO SPUN AROUND, Nico yipped and ran to her arms. Still holding Nico, Amparo sank onto the nearest chair.

"Wh-what just happened? Who did this?" She stared at the wall, at the chair, then at Javi, who stood paralyzed and white faced. For a few moments, no one spoke. The only sounds were of Nico whimpering, the refrigerator humming, and the faucet drip-drip-dripping into the sink.

"Nico?" Amparo peeled the little boy away from her chest. "Did you kick the chair in any way to make it slide back and hit the wall?"

Nico seemed surprised at the question and shook his head.

"Did you—did you do something to the plate?"

Nico shook his head and buried it back in her chest.

As she held Nico, Amparo's gaze drifted back to

99

the toppled chair and to the bits of china on the floor. Slowly she shifted her gaze to Javi. Her face wore a strange look.

"Javi, did you do this?"

Javi's jaw dropped. "Me? Did you not see what happened?"

Amparo shook her head. "I was looking for the Parmesan . . ."

"Why should I do such a thing?"

"You could have staged this to make me believe your ghost theory."

"How? I have not moved. The chair was across the table! The plate, too!"

"I noticed you doing something under the table with your foot a little while ago—"

"I give Nico a small kick. To make him pay attention. That is all."

"Perhaps a string—"

"There is no string. Look!" Javi held out his arms, palms up; he stepped in front of her and turned slowly so she could inspect him. He pulled his pockets inside out.

Amparo gently lifted Nico off her lap and set him down. She stepped to the chair. Crouching beside it, she examined its legs and back, apparently feeling for strings or anything else that might have been attached to the chair. Gingerly she picked up a piece of broken china.

Javi shook his head incredulously. "Why do you blame me? It is not I who push that chair. It is not Nico who throw the plate. It is Hamish!"

Amparo looked up. Her eyes held an expression of intense pain. She looked tired, older.

"Go to your room, Javi," she said softly. "And please

take Nico with you. I have to think. I need some time alone."

"Cricket crackers!" said Willo. Javi had ridden to her house to tell her what had happened the previous evening. "The chair just slid across the floor? All by itself?"

Javi nodded.

"And the plate flew off the table?"

Again he nodded.

"But nothing else moved? You didn't feel an earthquake or anything?"

"No, nothing."

The two fell silent for a few moments, then Willo said, "I've been thinking about those earthquakes you guys felt. Seems weird that they weren't reported on the news. Maybe we should call the seismology lab at Lawrence Berkeley Labs and ask if there have been any earthquakes in the last week."

"And if there have been no earthquakes?"

"Then maybe it was something else. Some force strong enough to shake the floor and the walls of your house. Maybe a paranormal force."

Javi considered her suggestion. "A force . . . yes, that is possible."

"Come on in." Willo pushed open the front door. "We can call now, if you like. Then we can ride to the library. I need more books."

Willo's bright and airy home was luxurious in a comfortable, lived-in way. In contrast to Amparo's rustic-style, dark-wood home, everything in Willo's house was painted white or left a natural light-colored wood.

Javi followed Willo into her father's office. She closed

the door and grabbed the phone book. Javi perched at the edge of a leather recliner, watching Willo page through the phone book till she found what she needed. She jotted down a number, grabbed the phone, and dialed.

He listened to her ask whether there had been any earthquakes in their area in the past five days and watched her face turn from one of mild interest to excitement, then concern. Maybe she, too, had been hoping there was a conventional reason for the earthquakes that he, Nico, and Amparo had felt. But he could tell by her face that the scientist at the lab had not given her good news. She thanked the person and hung up.

Willo swept her long hair over one shoulder and sat at her father's desk.

"What did they say?" Javi asked, suspecting he already knew.

"I talked to a Dr. Jorgensen, and she said there hasn't been any notable seismologic activity in California for over a week." Willo leaned forward. With the somber expression of a doctor who is about to tell a patient he only has one month to live, she said, "Javi, whatever you guys felt, it was no earthquake."

"I am thinking," Javi said to Willo when they arrived at the library, "possibly you may help me do some . . . how you say"—Javi paused to find the right word—"studies on ghosts?"

"You mean research?"

Javi nodded. "Yes, research. May you help me?"

" '*Will* you help me.' Sure. They've got a great parapsychology section here."

"And may—will—you read them and tell me about them? Tití Amparo will not allow me to—"

"Cripes! That's right! And if anyone needs to learn more about the paranormal, it's you."

"You do not mind?"

"Are you kidding? This is the kind of stuff I love to read about. Follow me."

Willo selected several books on psychic phenomena and the paranormal. They were thick, heavy books, and Javi was grateful that Willo, and not he, would be the one wading through them.

As they were about to head to the loan desk to check out the books, Javi remembered the summer reading program.

"Willo, did you think more about the summer reading program?"

"*Hmm?* No, not really."

Javi shifted awkwardly from foot to foot. "Will you? Think about it, I mean?"

"What about it?"

"Well . . . Tití says I must participate."

"Oh. Amparo's making you apply, and you don't want to?"

"Yes, and I thought—" He paused, wondering how to continue.

"Would you like me to sign up, so you will have a friendly face with you?"

Javi gave her a sheepish half smile. "Would you?"

Willo shrugged. "Sure, why not? I can always stick to the young adult books, if I find the easier books boring. Okay, let's do it. The best part is that Ms. Snow is leading the group, not Ms. Watkins."

When they reached the loan desk, Willo filled out the reading program form. "Don't you want to fill out the form?" she asked Javi.

"I already did. Tití has given it to Ms. Snow."

After Willo checked out their books, she went to look for Ms. Snow, to give her the form, and left Javi guarding the books.

"Well, if it isn't Javier."

The shrill voice tensed the muscles in Javi's neck. He turned slowly.

"How nice to see you again!" Ms. Watkins gave Javi a honey-sweet smile.

"Hello, Ms. Watkins."

The woman was wearing a shiny, banana yellow dress, so tight it looked like spray-painted enamel. Her red curls were pulled into a perky ponytail near the top of her head.

She eyed Javi with interest. "You know, I just can't believe, with those blue eyes and that light skin, that you're Puerto Rican."

Javi's backbone stiffened. "You think I lie?"

"No, of course—I didn't mean . . . I know! One of your parents must have been American."

Javi felt his ears grow warm. "They were both American. Puerto Rico is a commonwealth. All Puerto Ricans are citizens of the United States." Why did this woman insist on asking such stupid questions?

"Oh yes, of course . . . I just meant . . . white. Perhaps one of your parents was white."

"White?" Javi was shocked. So that was it. This stupid woman must think all Puerto Ricans were the same as the few she'd once met.

Javi pushed out his chin and looked her in the eye. "They were both white," he said, struggling to keep his voice calm and firm. "In Puerto Rico we have whites, blacks, mestizos, even descendants of Indians—the same as in the United States."

"Oh, well, yes, I just meant—"

"Hi, Ms. Watkins." Willo grabbed Javi's arm. "Come on, Javi, we've got to run."

Willo picked up her books with one arm and pulled Javi with the other. He had never been so relieved to have a conversation interrupted.

"Oh," said Ms. Watkins, "is your father outside waiting, Willo?" She glanced expectantly at the door.

"No, but Amparo will be waiting at my house if we don't hurry. Gotta go."

"See you next time, children."

As they ran out the door, Willo muttered, "Not if we see you first!"

20

"WHERE ARE WE GOING NOW?" Javi asked Amparo after they had spent most of the day selecting bedroom furniture for his and Nico's rooms. Now that she'd finished grading term papers and final exams, Amparo was keeping her promise to help the boys redecorate.

"To choose paint and wallpaper," she said, pulling up to the paint store.

"Do we get to choose our own?" Javi took Nico's hand and followed Amparo to the wallpaper section.

"Of course. Just remember, light colors like ecru or off-white make the room look bigger. Busy wallpaper makes the room seem smaller."

Javi paged through the huge wallpaper books, getting ideas from the photographs. Tired of the cramped room he shared with Nico, Javi wanted his room to feel as big as possible. He tried to picture his computer, his swimming trophies, and the other things from home in his new room.

"I think I would like something simple. Perhaps a thin strip of wallpaper trim near the top of my walls—like this." Javi showed Amparo a picture. "Then I can paint one wall forest green and the other three ecru to keep the room light. My shelves and swimming trophies can go on the green wall."

"Good choice," said Amparo. "I like that." After a moment she added, "I also like how well your English is coming along. You've worked very hard."

Javi looked down and shrugged.

Giving his shoulder a squeeze, Amparo said, "I want you to know how proud I am of you."

"¡Mira, mira!" cried Nico, pointing to a photograph of a child's room done in jungle decor. "I want a room just like this."

"Hmm," Amparo said, studying the picture. "Maybe I can make curtains from the matching fabric. Says here we can order it with the wallpaper. Would you like that, Nico?"

Nico hopped up and down, nodding with delight.

"Would you like to use the same colors as in the picture? Lime green with orange and yellow contrasts?"

Nico bounced and nodded again.

"And I can make a matching seat cushion for the top of the toy chest we ordered you. Would you like that?"

Nico ran in a circle, nodding madly and swinging Pulito by one leg over his head.

Amparo and Javi looked at each other and burst into laughter.

When he was done choosing, Nico entertained himself by lying on the floor and paging through oversized interior-design books. Soon he fell asleep, giving Amparo and Javi plenty of time to finish their selections.

"I'll need to order your curtains, Javi. Then I'll order matching bedspreads, sheets, and pillowcases for each of you."

"I do not want cute animals or other baby patterns," Javi said.

"Okay, how about these plaids? They complement the colors you chose for your room."

Once everything had been ordered, the major work began. Amparo and Javi set up shelves in the garage to hold all the boxes and other items she had been storing in the two rooms that would now be the boys' bedrooms.

When they had cleared the rooms of her stuff, Amparo showed Javi how to paint the walls and the wood trim. While she painted Nico's room, Javi painted his own. In less than a week both rooms were painted and wallpapered.

Slowly Javi's room was beginning to feel his own, to look like he lived there. He was proud of the job he'd done painting it. He'd been as meticulous with the walls and wood trim as he was with his sketches and watercolors. He'd lined up the thin roll of wallpaper trim just so, making sure it was straight and all the ends were even.

His room looked almost complete—almost. But he still needed a few posters for the walls, and bulletin boards that he could fill with his paintings, sketches, and souvenirs. Amparo took him to the malls in downtown Walnut Creek and Concord so he could find the very best posters. And when they got home, she helped him put them up.

In the midst of all the redecorating, Javi decided that his aunt really must want them to stay. She wouldn't have gone to all this work and expense if she was just going to keep them for a few months—until another relative volunteered to take them in—would she?

"Crocs on a rock!" Willo said, looking from wall to wall. After the final pieces of furniture arrived—Javi's desk, hutch, and bookshelves—Willo had been invited for the unveiling. "You guys did an incredible job!"

Amparo stood behind Javi and placed her hands on his shoulders. "I had nothing to do with Javi's room. He did all of this himself."

Javi felt a warm glow, a sensation he hadn't experienced since his parents died. "Tití helped with the wallpaper and the posters," he confessed, grinning up at her. "And she's the one who taught me to paint the walls."

"But you chose the colors and the decor, and you did all the work. You should feel very proud." Still standing behind him, Amparo kissed the top of his head. Then she wrapped her arms around his chest and gave him a hearty squeeze.

Javi placed his arms over hers, enjoying the feel of them. Then, realizing Willo was watching, he said, "Come see Nico's room, Willo. Tití just finished the curtains."

He led her to the room next to his—the room he used to share with Nico.

"Crickets!" Willo said when she entered Nico's room. "You made these curtains, Amparo? They look positively professional."

"Thanks, but I'm not about to change careers. I thought sewing curtains would be easy. Next time I'll pay the extra and have a real professional do them."

The children laughed at Amparo's wiped-out expression, then turned to admire Nico's room. One large wall was papered with a jungle scene that matched the scene in the curtains, bedspread, and pillow shams—orange tigers, yellow lions, large green palm trees, and exotic birds populated the scene. The other three walls were painted a pale lime green. A small wooden table and four tiny chairs sat under the window, and a desk and matching bookshelves lined another wall. The decor brightened the room considerably, and without all of Amparo's storage boxes, the room looked much larger.

Nico was obviously thrilled with his tiny table and chairs, where he sat coloring.

"What are you drawing, Nico?" Willo asked, stepping next to him. "How do you say that in Spanish, Javi?"

"I understand," Nico said in English, and held up his sketch pad.

The page showed a scene full of green squiggles that appeared to be palm leaves. In the center, a yellow oval with a circle-head and four stick legs trotted behind another oval-and-stick-legged animal, drawn in orange. The orange oval had black slashes drawn across it. They seemed to be a yellow lion and an orange tiger, like the ones on Nico's wallpaper. Atop the lion rode a little brown-haired stick figure, and on the tiger rode a yellow-haired stick figure.

Nico pointed, and in perfect English, he said, "See, Nico and Hamish live in the jungle. Together."

JAVI FELT AS THOUGH he'd stepped into a freezer.

Hamish was back.

Javi had hoped that keeping Nico busy the past week helping with little chores, and ignoring Hamish, would make the ghost simply go away on his own. But now Javi realized the opposite must have happened. Left mostly on his own while Javi and Amparo worked, Nico had had extra time to be alone with Hamish.

Enough time to learn more English.

Enough time to become more attached to a ghost.

All the anger and frustration that Javi had been freed from for the past week returned with renewed force. "What do you mean, you and Hamish live together in the jungle?"

"Here, in my jungle room," Nico replied. "We will live here."

"Hamish is going to sleep in this room, too?"

"*Mm-hmm.*" Nico got up and pulled the hidden trundle bed from under his bed. "See, now that you have your own room, he sleeps here."

Javi turned to Amparo. "I do not like this, Tití. I do not like this at all."

"Let it go, Javi," Amparo said. She gave him that firm, warning look he had learned meant she was going to send him to his room if he pushed further. "We'll talk about it later."

"But, Tití—"

"I mean it, Javi."

Willo placed a hand on his shoulder. He could tell she was also warning him not to push the matter further. It made him angrier to have the two of them ganging up on him, even if he knew Willo's reason was different from his aunt's. He shrugged her hand off his shoulder and scowled at Amparo.

Javi clenched his fists. "Tití, I keep trying to tell you—"

The lights in Nico's room flickered, then switched off for a few seconds and back on. The moment the lights came on, the stereo in Javi's room began to blare a heavy-metal song that shook the walls. The loud bass rumbled through the floor and vibrated up their legs.

Javi ran into his room and turned it off. The lights in his room flickered, then switched on and off. The numbers on his digital clock raced as if adjusted by an invisible hand. The stereo blared again, but this time on a Hispanic station. Salsa music rattled the windows.

"Javi!" Amparo called. "Turn that thing off!"

Javi tried again. "I did, but—"

Downstairs the TV blasted the news throughout the house. Fidel barked and the cats screeched.

"What in the—?" Amparo flew past his door and down

the hall. The hall lights flicked on and off as she ran. Within a few moments the TV was silenced, and Javi could hear his aunt shushing the pets.

Willo, who had been comforting Nico, ran into Javi's room carrying the little boy on one hip. "Do you think . . . ?"

Before Javi could reply, Fidel began to bark again.

Javi pushed past Willo and raced downstairs, with Willo and Nico close behind.

"Hush, Fidel! Quiet, boy." Amparo's voice was coming from the kitchen.

"What happened?" Javi asked as he ran in.

Amparo was standing by the sink. At her feet Fidel crouched, growling.

"I don't know," she said, pushing her hair back from her forehead. "The television was going great guns, and when I turned it off, the garbage disposal turned on. I wonder if—"

At that moment a humming, whirling, thumping noise escaped from the laundry room. The kids followed Amparo to the laundry-room door. The dryer was humming and shaking from side to side. The little Scottie guarded the doorway, barking and growling as loudly as a Great Dane.

"This stupid old dryer." Amparo turned off the dryer and checked inside. It was empty. "Be quiet, Fidel! Javi, did you try to use the dryer earlier today?"

"No, not today. But if I had, why would it turn on now?"

"I don't know," Amparo replied, sounding more annoyed than frightened. "I just hope the electrical in this house isn't going out on us. After all the redecorating, another big expense would be tough."

As if on cue, the lights in the kitchen and laundry room

began switching on and off. The dishwasher came alive, churning and chugging. Fidel dashed to the dishwasher and bounced in front of it, yipping and snapping.

Amparo gave a frustrated sigh and shut off the dishwasher. "Be quiet, Fidel! Javi, could you get me Bert Albertson's number from the phone list on the fridge? He's a good electrician. Maybe he can get to the bottom of this. While I call him, would you and Willo take Fidel outside? He's making me crazy."

"I think maybe I did something wrong when I turned off the electricity this morning to wire the dimmer switches in the boys' rooms," Amparo said to Bert when he arrived an hour later.

"I wouldn't be surprised." Bert, a large, round man, towered over Amparo. The few wisps of white hair he had left sprouted at the edges of a very bald head. "Why didn't you call me, Doc? You shouldn't be taking your life in your hands, working with electrical wires. That's what I'm trained for."

"It was two simple switches, Bert."

"Maybe. And maybe you just fouled up all your electrical."

"Bert, I can't afford—"

"Don't you worry. Have I ever cheated you?"

"Well, no . . ."

"Then don't worry. Now show me where the problem is."

Javi and Willo followed them into the kitchen. As soon as they entered, the lights began to flicker and turn on and off.

"Ooo-weee!" said Bert, rubbing his shiny head. "I shore

never seen anything like this. What'd you do to your electrical, little lady?"

"That's what I hope you can figure out, Bert."

"Well, let me mosey on out and take a look at the circuit breakers. If anyone can fix this, I'm your man."

"I certainly hope so," Amparo muttered as Bert disappeared into the garage.

"Tití," said Javi, "are you sure it is an electrical problem?"

"Of course, Javi, what else—"

Javi's furrowed brows and the look in his eyes told her what else.

She shook her head vigorously and held up her hand. "Oh no, Javi. Not this again. We haven't had any problems for over a week. And I've warned you, I don't want to hear any more about hauntings."

"I was hoping the strange things had stopped. But now—"

Willo placed a hand on his shoulder. "Maybe Amparo is right, Javi. Maybe this is only an electrical problem."

"Perhaps," Javi replied grudgingly, "but it is a very strange one." He couldn't believe Willo and his aunt couldn't see what was perfectly plain to him. It was so frustrating!

The lights switched off and the hum from the refrigerator died. Bert poked his head in the kitchen door.

"Don't worry, folks. I just turned off the juice at the circuit-breaker panel. Gotta make sure the electricity in the kitchen's off so's I can run some—" The lights flickered back on and stayed on. Bert glanced around and scratched his head. "Well, I'll be gal-durned! I could've sworn I turned it off. Be right back."

Bert headed back to the garage.

The refrigerator hummed back to life, the lights flickered, then the refrigerator was silent and the lights died. Bert came back in the house, scratching his head and tugging his few wisps of hair, which now stuck straight out above his ears.

"I just don't get it. I'd turned the kitchen breakers off, all right. And everything looks good out there. No fuses blown, no circuits popped. Let me just see—" The kitchen lights, as well as those in the hall and living room, began to switch on and off. "Well, I'll be a five-legged horned toad! What the dickens have you done, Doc?"

Willo ran upstairs to check the bedrooms. "The lights in Nico's and Javi's rooms are going wild again," she called out from the top of the stairs.

Bert pulled at a tuft of hair above his left ear. "I guess I'll just have to shut off the main circuit breakers—kill the juice to the whole house. Durndest thing I ever saw," he muttered as he waddled off to the backyard, wagging his head.

After a few minutes all the lights went out and the entire house was silent. Bert came back in, muttering under his breath.

"Listen, Bert," said Amparo, grabbing her purse and car keys, "I'll be back in an hour. I almost forgot my dentist appointment. If I'm not back before you're done, just leave the bill with Javi. Javi and Willo—"

"You must leave now?" Javi couldn't believe his aunt's timing.

"Javi, I have to. It's too late to cancel. Will you—?"

Javi sighed. "Fine. We will care for Nico, Tití." Javi handed her the cell phone. "Do not worry."

As soon as Amparo's car backed out of the garage, the TV in the living room flipped on to the news channel, at maximum volume.

Bert jumped as if he'd been struck by lightning. "Well, I'll be—" He ran to turn off the TV set and pulled the plug to be safe. When he turned around, still holding the plug, the volume came back on and the screen flipped from channel to channel. Bert dropped the plug and dashed back to the kitchen. The TV went dead.

"D-did you see that?" he asked, peering from the kitchen door at the television set.

Javi and Willo glanced questioningly at each other. Willo, holding Nico at her side, lifted an eyebrow. No one replied.

"I tell you, it's the durndest thing I ever saw!" Bert glanced around the kitchen and peeked out into the hall, tugging at the hair over his left ear. "Well, things seem to have settled down. Let me do some checking around. I'd better go upstairs and take a look at them dimmer switches your aunt put in."

Bert side-stepped into the hall, glancing around as if he expected something to jump out at him. Then he bolted up the stairs.

Willo touched Javi's arm. "Javi—"

"*Shh*, wait. Come, sit."

"But shouldn't we follow Bert?"

"In a moment. *Siéntate*, Nico." Javi pulled out a chair for Nico.

The kids sat at the kitchen table. In the silent house, Javi could hear Bert slowly walking from room to room, floorboards squeaking under his weight. Then Javi couldn't hear him anymore.

"Willo," Javi whispered, "I do not believe as Tití say that this is an electrical problem, do you?"

"I—I don't know what it is . . . Did you see that TV set? It turned on even though it was unplugged. So it can't be just an electrical problem, not if the TV was unplugged."

"This is what I mean. I believe it is Hamish."

Nico tugged at Javi's sleeve. "But Hamish is not—," he began in a loud voice.

"*Shh,* Nico," Javi turned to his brother and placed his finger to his lips. He spoke in Spanish. "We must be very quiet. We don't want to disturb Mr. Bert."

Willo sighed. "It's just too bad Amparo wasn't here to see the TV turn on without being plugged in. Then she might be more willing to listen to your theory and to look at the unsolved mysteries book."

"Yes, very too bad." Javi shook his head, annoyed that Amparo had chosen this time to go to the dentist and miss all of Hamish's tricks. If she were here, she couldn't deny that what was happening was not normal—had no *logical* explanation. "Perhaps we should now go up—"

At that moment the kitchen lights flashed on and off in rapid succession. Javi glanced at the wall switch. As the lights flashed, the light switch flipped up and down as if controlled by an invisible hand.

Javi pointed. "Willo, look!"

Willo's eyes opened wide. Before she could say anything, Bert clumped through the upstairs hall and thundered down the stairs. He appeared in the kitchen pale-faced and glistening with sweat.

Javi stood up. "Did you find anything, Mr. Bert? Did my aunt cross a wire or make a mistake?"

Bert's gaze slid to the wall switch that controlled the

kitchen lights. He eyed it as if it were a poisonous snake and rubbed the top of his head. Javi had a feeling that when Bert was upstairs alone, he'd seen the switches flip up and down by themselves.

"No, sir. Can't say's I found anything wrong with the wiring. Tell the doc she did a right fine job . . . Something's wrong. Something's mighty wrong, but I'll be dit-durned if I can figure it out." Bert looked down at his heavy brown boots. He shifted his weight.

"Mr. Bert, did you see anything . . . very strange?" Javi asked.

A sudden strong draft made the white wisps above Bert's ears flap as gently as butterfly wings. He froze. Slowly his eyes, only his eyes, moved upward, gazing toward the ceiling.

The ceiling fan had turned on and was blowing cool air to the stunned spectators below.

Bert shook his head and rubbed his whole face with large, meaty hands. "Very strange? I'll say! Lights and fans flipping on and off with no juice going to them. TVs turning on when they're unplugged. Never seen anything like it."

"Do you think"—Javi paused—"perhaps you can tell my aunt—?"

"Tell your aunt? So she'll think I'm crazy? I don't think I'll ever tell anyone about this."

"But—"

Bert glanced at Javi but didn't look him in the eye. He shifted his weight again. "Sorry, young feller, not a thing I can do. Just tell your aunt the wiring, circuit breakers, main panel—everything looks fine. Wish I could help you. I'll turn on the main breakers on my way out."

He hurried to the garage door, making a gesture that looked like the sign of the cross and muttering, "Not that you need them. Your electrical has a mind of its own."

When Javi went to the door to lock it behind Bert, the man turned and whispered, "What you need is a priest."

JAVI'S EYES SNAPPED OPEN. He gazed around his new room, wondering what had wakened him. He glanced at the digital clock. Six-thirty—too early. He had had trouble getting to sleep last night, thinking about the electrical disturbances and about Bert's last comment. Now he felt exhausted.

So why was he awake?

He looked up at the window. The morning fog hung heavily, blocking out the sun and covering the tops of the trees. His room was dark and the house eerily quiet.

Something was wrong. He could feel it. He could feel it as strongly as he'd felt other things before—things that had come true. As strongly as he'd felt that the nightmare of his parents' car crash wasn't just a dream. As strongly as he'd known that if they went out in the car that morning, they wouldn't be coming back.

He remembered the nightmare he'd had his first night in California. His stomach lurched. There was that prickling sensation crawling like a spider up and down his spine. He pushed the covers off and sat up in bed. A magnetlike force pulled his gaze toward the window. His heart jerked.

Nico was on the footbridge, running toward the woods.

Javi shoved his feet into his slippers, grabbed his robe, and flew down the hall and out of the house. As he ran it occurred to him that Nico was probably with Hamish.

The thought of Hamish made his heart beat even harder. He was taking Nico somewhere, Javi just knew it. But where? And where was the evil thing? Was it still waiting in the woods?

In two steps Javi leaped over the footbridge and turned left, following the faint path that Nico had taken through the woods, the same path Javi had taken in his nightmare. He controlled the urge to call to his brother, fearing Nico might hide rather than be forced to return to the house.

Soon Javi spotted a red flash through a patch of leaves. He veered off the path and tore through the weeds. A red cap bobbed up and down behind the tall weeds. Javi made a beeline for the cap.

"Nico!" he cried, grabbing the little boy from behind and flinging him around. "Are you okay?"

Nico stared at him, dazed. He blinked and looked around.

"Are you okay?" Javi repeated.

Along with his red cap, Nico wore a jacket and woolen scarf over his pajamas, but he had a sleepy, dopey look, as if he had been sleepwalking. He rubbed his eyes and smiled. He nodded.

Nico's cap was turned backward and was slightly askew,

so the bill stuck out behind one ear. He looked so small and helpless. Javi grabbed him again and hugged him close. "You scared me, you know that?"

Nico giggled. "Javi *bobo*."

"Listen to me, Nico. This isn't funny. Remember what Tití said about going into the woods alone."

"I'm not alone. I'm with Hamish."

Javi was learning not to argue with Nico about Hamish. "Well, you and Hamish can't go into the woods alone, either. You can only come out here if someone is with you— Tití or I."

A crow cawed overhead, a nasty, screeching sound that made Javi's teeth feel as if someone had run fingernails across a chalkboard. Another crow returned the call. Javi looked up. Three large black birds flew from the top of a nearby oak and melted into the fog. A sudden chill wind came up.

"*Vente,* Nico. Let's hurry before Tití wakes up and notices we're gone." Javi took his little brother's hand and began leading him back to the house.

"Hamish!" Nico called, looking around. "Javi, I can't find Hamish."

"Hamish can take care of himself. He's been doing it long enough."

"No, Javi, he'll get lost." Nico struggled to pull free. "The evil one will get him if we leave him."

Javi tightened his grip. "Nico, hurry up. Hamish is probably at the house, waiting for you."

His own words sent shivers down his back. He hoped he was wrong. He hoped Hamish had gone away and would never come back.

As Javi hurried Nico along the ragged trail, the little

boy kept looking back, calling Hamish and whimpering. Javi quickened his pace. He had the same sensation he'd had the first day he'd been out near the woods walking Fidel.

Someone was watching.

He glanced over his shoulder and thought he saw a dark shadow, like black smoke, approaching through the trees. The wind came up again, shivering through the weeds and whispering in the leaves. Javi began to run, pulling Nico behind.

Nico cried out, stumbled on a tree root, and fell. Javi turned. The dark shadow was almost upon them. Javi scooped up his little brother and ran for the footbridge, leaping over it, then flew through the backyard, up the steps, and into the house. Holding Nico in one arm, he slid the door shut and leaned against it. His heart thumped like that of a hunted rabbit.

ZsaZsa and Misifú became streaks of white and gray as they dashed under the desk. With large, frightened eyes, they peeked out.

Fidel, who had been waiting by the glass door, curled his upper lip, showing his teeth, and growled from deep in his throat. He pounced at the door, snarling and barking.

Javi set Nico down and turned to look through the glass. A shimmery image seemed to hover in front of the old oak near the footbridge, warping the tree the way a wave of heat rising from hot coals or hot pavement distorts the area behind it. The image lingered for a moment and began to dissipate. Soon nothing remained but a slight breeze that rustled the leaves of the oak. Then even the leaves were still.

Willo was right.

Something wicked *was* in those woods.

"HURRY UP, JAVI," Willo called. "What's wrong? Don't you want to go in?"

Amparo had dropped Javi and Willo off at the library for the first meeting of the summer reading program. As they walked toward the front door, Javi hung back, turning to wave good-bye to Nico and Amparo, retying his shoes, checking out the weather.

"I do not care," he said, shrugging.

Willo grinned. "Don't worry, it's going to be fun. You'll see. You'll do just fine."

"I know. It is no problem."

"So, c'mon. Let's sneak by the loan desk so we can avoid old Carrot Locks."

Javi heaved a deep sigh and followed her. He wasn't sure why he was resisting the reading group so much. Maybe it was having to speak English to other kids—kids who might not be as nice as Willo if he made mistakes. Kids who might make fun of his accent.

Willo stopped just inside the main entrance and peered around the corner. "So far all's clear. She's probably haunting the stacks. Keep an eye out for her."

Willo led him to a small room he'd never seen before. The door was closed, but through the window, he could see tables and chairs and four kids about his age sitting around chatting. Two boys and two girls.

The moment they entered, the talking ceased and four pairs of eyes stared. Javi's intestines turned to Jell-O.

"Hey there, Will-o'-the-Wisp," said a beefy, red-faced boy. "Who's your new friend?"

"Here, Willo." A tiny blond girl grabbed something off one of the tables and handed it to Willo. "They made name tags for us. At first I thought it was silly—as if we didn't all know each other, right? But I guess it wasn't such a bad idea." Her large blue eyes fixed on Javi's face. She gave him a shy smile.

Javi tried to smile back, but his lips were numb.

"Thanks, Kimberly." Willo pinned her name tag to her sweatshirt and handed Javi his.

Javi took the plastic tag and stared at it as if he'd never seen such a thing in his life. His first name was printed in large black letters: JAVI.

Willo whispered, "You're supposed to pin it on."

Javi looked up and realized everyone was staring at him again. His neck felt hot and sweaty. He tried to pin the name tag to his T-shirt. First he stuck the pin in his chest, then he pricked his thumb. He tried not to wince.

The red-faced boy stepped forward. "*Huh*, there's an interesting name. Javi, like Java Man."

"It's pronounced 'Havi,' you moron," Willo said. "Short for Javier. The *j* in Spanish is pronounced like an *h*."

"Sorry, Your Royal Willowiness." The boy bowed, as if he were begging her pardon.

The blond girl stepped in front of the red-faced boy. "Ignore Robert, Javi, everyone tries to. It's nice to meet you. I'm Kimberly, see?" She pointed to her name tag as proof. "That's Amy with the brown curls, and the bald cue ball with the hoop in his ear is Max."

Javi glanced awkwardly at everyone.

"So when are we getting started?" Willo asked. "Isn't it time?"

"One of the librarians came to tell us to be patient. It seems they're running late."

Javi's stomach sank. He didn't relish being stuck in a small room with a group of strange kids who might choose him as the next suitable topic of conversation.

"I will be back, Willo," he whispered. "I go to the rest room."

Javi bolted out the door. He dashed to the rest room and splashed water on his face. He glanced at his watch. He wished he could stay in there until it was time to leave, but he knew that Willo or Ms. Snow would send one of the boys to get him. He didn't want Robert or Max to catch him hiding in the bathroom like a baby.

Javi waited five minutes, then headed back to the conference room. Taking a deep breath, he pulled the spring-loaded door. He froze.

Ms. Watkins, wearing a skintight jungle-print mini-dress, stood before the group. She had apparently been speaking for a few minutes. ". . . But I now have some good news and some bad news. The bad news is that Ms. Snow has broken her hip and is still in the hospital. The good news is that I will be your new program director."

Javi released the door and stepped forward. The full weight of the spring-loaded door slammed into him, whacking him on the head. The loud *thump* made everyone turn around. Javi stumbled forward and fell to his knees.

"Javi!" Ms. Watkins and Willo ran to his aid.

"Are you all right, Javi?" Ms. Watkins's voice sounded two octaves higher than usual.

"Yes, I—I am all right." He winced. His head throbbed. He rubbed it.

"You're hurt," said Willo. "The door hit your head."

Javi looked up. This time six pairs of eyes were staring at him. "No, please. I am fine. I will possibly have a small cardinal on my head tomorrow. That is all."

Snorts and snickers erupted around the room. Willo bit her lips together, but Javi could tell she, too, wanted to laugh.

"A cardinal on your head?" cried Robert. "Is that the Mexican cure for a bad headache?"

"Shut up, moron," Willo said. "Come on, Javi, come sit down."

"What did I say?" Javi whispered. "Did I say something wrong?"

"I'm not sure what you meant to say, but I don't think you said what you meant."

Javi's ears burned. He took a seat at the back of the room, against the wall. Willo sat next to him. He stared at his desk. He couldn't bear to meet her eyes.

The other four participants were still laughing. Robert was snickering about cardinals on the head and bats in the belfry.

"Ignore them, Javi," Willo whispered. "You know how some kids can be real jerks."

Javi shrugged. "I do not care. I do not listen to them."

Ms. Watkins managed to calm down the group and to start a discussion about each person's favorite type of book. As each person talked, Ms. Watkins took notes. Javi refused to participate. He avoided the woman's eyes when she scanned the group for volunteers.

"I like dog stories and horse stories." Kimberly glanced back at Javi. "Anything to do with animals, really. I want to be a vet when I grow up."

"Thank you, Kimberly," said Ms. Watkins. "We have several dog books this season. Some are even told from the dog's point of view. Won't that be interesting? Amy, how about you?"

"I *love* historical fiction."

Ms. Watkins nodded. "Good, good. Now let me see, Robert wants science fiction; Max likes adventures and *no* books about girls; Kimberly wants animal books; Amy, historical fiction; and Willo prefers horror and ghost stories but will read anything with a girl protagonist. So far each of you has a different taste. So there won't be any arguing over who gets what." She giggled. "Javi, what kind of books do you like?"

Javi shrugged. He would like horror and ghost stories, too, but Amparo would not allow those. Maybe adventures, like Max, or historical fiction, like Amy, or even science fiction. No, mysteries. No one had asked for mysteries yet. Yes, perhaps mysteries.

He tried to speak. All six pairs of eyes seemed to be boring holes in his body. He looked down. His face flushed. Now his tongue felt like it had swollen to the size of a large sponge. He shrugged again, afraid to risk any kind of speech.

"Okay," said Ms. Watkins. "You think about it, and we'll come back to you later. How's that?"

Javi nodded and sank down in his chair.

In the meantime Ms. Watkins pulled some books from a box on her desk. She divided them into piles, then took one from each pile and began handing them out.

"Javi, until you decide, I've selected a very nice book for you." She placed a book on Javi's desk.

"Class, these books are called advance reading samples. Publishers send us only one copy of each of these, so please be very careful with them. They are intended as promotionals—to give librarians, such as myself, an opportunity to read the book without purchasing it. Then, if we like the book, we can order several copies of it.

"Each of you is to take one book home per week. You will read the book and be ready to report on it at the next meeting. Then we will hear your report and discuss the book. We want you to give us a thorough critique—be specific about what you like and don't like. If two or more of you finish a book early, you may exchange books with someone else. We want as many of you as possible to read each book. Finally we will all vote on the books that are worth spending precious library funds to buy.

"This program serves two purposes: First, it will expose each of you to excellent literature. Second, it will help the librarians, because we don't have enough time to read all the books we are sent, and it will tell us which books children will enjoy. Libraries don't have many funds these days, so we want to be sure to buy only the best books—books many people will enjoy."

As Ms. Watkins rambled on, Javi examined the book on his desk. The cover showed the face of an Asian boy about his age. He fanned through the pages. Small type, long paragraphs, very, very long chapters, and worst of all, it was full of big English words he could barely pronounce. *Ay!* This would not be at all fun! He would have to read day and night to finish this in one week!

He glanced again at the cover. What had made Ms. Watkins think he would enjoy this book?

"So what were you trying to say—when you said you'd have a cardinal on your head tomorrow?" Willo asked Javi during their fifteen-minute break. The others had left the room to go to the rest room or to grab a snack.

Javi shot her a glance. Her eyes were dancing, but her expression was as solemn as that of a priest delivering a eulogy.

"I do not understand," he said. "What is so funny?"

Willo leaned forward. "Tell me what 'cardinal on the head' means."

"You know. When you are hurt and you get a blue-and-purple spot on your skin."

"A bruise?"

"Bruise? In Spanish we say *cardenal*. What is a cardinal in English?"

Willo bit her lips again. Her eyes crinkled.

"You are laughing!" cried Javi.

"No, really"—Willo's shoulders shook—"I'm not. I—I just can't help it."

Javi stood up. "I am leaving."

"No, wait." Willo pulled him back down. "It's just that . . . a cardinal is a type of bird—a red bird. 'Cardinal' also means a high-ranking Catholic priest, like a bishop—the one who wears the red robes."

"A bird?" Javi swallowed. "Or a priest?" Of course. In Spanish, *cardenal* means a red bird or a high-ranking priest, too. But it also means a bruise. He had just assumed the same was true of the English word "cardinal."

Javi groaned. He had told the whole group that he would have a red bird or a priest on his head tomorrow. He stood back up.

"Now where are you going?" Willo followed him out the door.

"I must leave before the others come back. I cannot look at them."

"No, Javi. You can't leave. If you leave now, Robert will never let you live it down. He's a pig, but he's a smart pig, and he's going to be in all our classes next year. You can't show him you're upset by this."

Javi closed his eyes. She was right. Anyway, Tití Amparo would never let him get out of attending the stupid reading program.

He pulled the door open and stepped back in the room.

24

"JAVI?" LATE THE NEXT MORNING Amparo tapped on his door and poked her head inside.

Javi had been struggling through his novel from the reading group. It was an interesting story about a young Cambodian boy who, like Javi, had lost his parents and had come to the United States to live with a relative. Javi found he could easily relate to the boy's problems. This was the part he liked. He would tell this to the class as part of his critique, if he could ever find the courage to speak up.

But it was such a long book! That was the part he did *not* like. He had read two hours last night, and one hour this morning, and he had only finished twenty pages—he hadn't even finished the first chapter.

Also, it seemed he had read more of his dictionary than of his novel. In three hours he could finish at least half a book this length in Spanish. Would reading English *ever* get easier?

"Are you getting ready to take a bath?" said Amparo.

"Bath?" Javi glanced up from his book. "No, I took a shower when I got up."

Amparo's face wore a puzzled frown. "That's what I thought, but someone turned on the water in the upstairs bathtub. If I hadn't heard it, the tub would have overflowed."

"Did you ask Nico? Perhaps he wanted to float his new sailboat."

"Good idea." Amparo popped her head into the hallway. "Nico? Come here, please."

Javi heard Nico's chair legs scrape the floor and the soft padding sounds of running feet. "*Sí*, Tití?"

"Nico, *m'ijo*, did you turn on the water in the bathtub?"

Nico smiled up at her and shook his head.

Amparo frowned. "Did Hamish?"

Again Nico shook his head.

"Are you very sure?"

"Hamish and I have been coloring in my room. We haven't gone to the bathroom."

A sudden chill tingled Javi's arms. If neither Nico nor Hamish had turned on the water, who had?

Amparo sighed. "Nico, come sit beside Javi on his bed. Okay, *muchachos*, enough is enough. There are only three of us in this house. Someone turned on the faucet in the upstairs bathtub and let it run. If I hadn't gone by and heard it, the tub would have overflowed. I don't have to tell you how serious the damage to the floor and ceiling would have been, do I?"

Javi felt his face flush. "Tití, I do not know who turned it on. I have told you I did not do it. Why would I do such a thing?"

Amparo ran her fingers through her hair. "Well, I don't know. Perhaps you're still—"

"Maybe it was Fidel," Nico offered.

"No, Nico. It was not Fidel or ZsaZsa or Misifú. Pets cannot turn on the water in the tub. And you should never turn on the bath water by yourself, Nico. Even to float your sailboat. You must always call me or Javi to help you. Understand?"

Nico nodded.

Amparo turned to Javi. "Javi, if you turn on the water, you must remember that you did so. This is not a game, *muchachos*. The damage to the house would have been very expensive to repair."

"But I didn't—"

"Javi—"

"Do you not hear what I have said? Strange things begin to happen again. First the electricity, now this. And still you do not believe. Instead you blame us."

"That's enough, Javi. I'm not accusing either one of you—this time. But nothing like this had better happen again."

Soon after the bathtub incident, Amparo rounded up the boys to help her weed the yard. It was a cool, overcast day—perfect for yard work, she proclaimed. Javi half suspected she was trying to keep their minds and fingers busy to keep them out of trouble. But he was glad to have any excuse to take a break from his book.

Amparo assigned Javi the task of pulling dandelion leaves and crabgrass from the back lawn; she would do the same for the front lawn. Nico would pull obvious weeds from the flower beds along the borders. She taught them both how to pull the weeds so no roots remained behind, then she left them to go work in the front.

As Javi worked, pushing the tiny spade Amparo had given him down below the dandelions' roots and firmly pulling up the weeds, he kept glancing over his shoulder at the spot beyond the footbridge. He shuddered, remembering the shimmering image from the other morning. Even the pets had known something evil was hovering . . . just beyond the bridge.

It suddenly occurred to him that Fidel and the cats acted differently around Hamish than they did toward the evil thing. The cats either ignored Hamish or regarded him with bored expressions, and Fidel seemed quite fond of the little ghost. But each time Fidel sensed the evil one, he'd growl and bare his teeth. And that morning the cats had been terrified.

Maybe he was wrong. Maybe Hamish was not dangerous. If he were, the animals would sense it, wouldn't they? Maybe he should feel sorry for, rather than threatened by, the little ghost who had once been a frightened child, also missing his parents.

But no . . . something wasn't right. He felt it in his gut. Who had shoved the chair and thrown the plate against the wall the night of their spaghetti dinner? Who had been playing with the electricity? And who had left the water running in the bathtub this morning? Were these the playful acts of a childish spirit, or were they the beginning of some sinister attack from a more ominous force?

The cawing of a crow made him look up and glance toward Nico. The little boy was gone.

Javi spun around and saw him pulling weeds by the footbridge.

"Nico! Get away from there! Come back near the house. Look, there are lots of weeds around the flowers next to the house. Come on."

"Hamish wants to play in the stream. He likes the water."

Javi ran to Nico's side and yanked him away from the stream. He glanced nervously at the old oak, just beyond the bridge. "Hamish can play wherever he wants. We have no time to play right now. Tití wants us to pull these stupid weeds. *Vente,* come on."

He herded Nico in front of him and got him settled pulling weeds near the house.

"Nico," he said, helping his brother pull a few weeds from the flower bed, "I thought Hamish was afraid to go near the woods. Why does he want to play near the woods today?"

"The evil one isn't there right now. Sometimes he goes away. Then Hamish tries to find his parents."

"His parents?"

"Yes. Hamish needs to find his parents. He wants to go home."

An ice-cold hand clamped Javi's heart. He remembered his nightmare of Nico lost in the woods. And he remembered the other morning—the terror he had felt when he awoke to find Nico gone and believed the nightmare had come true. He grabbed his little brother's shoulders and squeezed. "Nico, don't you ever, *ever* go off with Hamish alone. Not to find his parents, not to play in the stream, not to do anything. Do you hear me?"

Nico struggled to pull away. "*Ay,* Javi, you're hurting me."

Javi let go. "I'm sorry, I—"

A shriek pierced the air, followed by a long, loud scream.

The gate at the side of the house slammed open, and Amparo stormed into the yard.

She was drenched from head to toe. Her hair, soaked and plastered to her head, dripped onto her hunched shoulders. Her shirt and jeans clung to her body. Water from her clothes formed a small puddle under her shoes that spread outward along the concrete path.

She looked as wet as if she had been dropped from the bench in a dunking booth at a fair, and just as angry. Her eyes blazed. She glowered at the boys, first at one, then at the other, as if one of them had thrown the winning ball that had dunked her.

"Okay, which one of you turned on the front-lawn sprinklers?"

"Javi, Nico! Get down here this instant!"

Amparo's voice pulled Javi's concentration away from the novel about the Cambodian boy. He was just getting to a good part, too. Javi closed his eyes and took a deep breath.

Slowly he rose from the chair and stepped to his door. He had managed to convince Amparo that neither of the boys had left the backyard or had gone anywhere near any sprinkler controls. Once she thought about it, Amparo decided it must have been another fluke, probably attributable to the still faulty electrical system. So what could be wrong now?

Nico zipped past, padding softly in his white socks. He glanced back and beckoned Javi. "Hurry, Javi. Tití called."

"I heard." Javi sauntered down the hall, in no particular hurry to see what he would be accused of next.

As soon as he entered the living room, Javi could tell something was wrong. Amparo, tense faced and tight lipped, paced the floor without acknowledging their presence. When both boys were seated on the couch, she began to speak and continued to pace as though she were lecturing a class.

"Just a few hours after this morning's bathtub incident, and now I find the faucets in the kitchen and in the downstairs bathroom left running and unattended. Fortunately the sinks did not back up, so they didn't flood. But that is no excuse. This is not a game, and this is not amusing.

"I've tried to reason with you. I've tried to give you the benefit of the doubt. But there are only three of us in this house. I know I didn't turn on those faucets, and—no matter what someone is trying to prove—they do not turn on by themselves. That leaves one of you two." Amparo paused, looked each boy in the eye, then resumed pacing.

"I'm a trained psychologist, and I've tried to look at this situation as a professional. I've asked myself, What could possibly make one of the boys do such a thing? And I came up with several possibilities. One"—Amparo held up a finger—"perhaps he is feeling unwanted and needs to test my limits. But how could that be? I asked myself. I have done everything I can think of to make them both feel wanted. I try to cook the meals they like, even though I hate to cook. I let them participate in redecorating their rooms, so they feel that the rooms are truly theirs. So, no, I tell myself, it cannot be that they still feel unwanted.

"Possibility number two"—still pacing, Amparo held up two fingers—"perhaps he has decided to be rebellious to gain my attention. But again I think, How can this be? I have showered both boys with attention. Once my classes were over, I spent over a week taking them shopping for furniture and paint and wallpaper. We spent hours and hours together. Every day I make sure to spend several hours with each of you. If anything, I would think you'd be tired of having your old aunt around so much. So what could it be?

"Perhaps number three—" Amparo held up three fingers, then she balled up her fists and brought her hands to her face. She stood still. "Perhaps he thinks I do not love him and is trying to see how much I can take. But"— Amparo's voice cracked; she turned to look at Javi and Nico—"if this is so, I do not know what more I can do to show you both how much I love you."

She sank to the floor in front of them. Her professional facade had crumpled, and she looked tired and sad. Sitting on her heels with her hands spread palms up, she said, "In the past few weeks, I've grown to love the two of you more than I ever thought possible. I've never had children, but I'm certain I couldn't love you more if you were my very own."

Amparo regarded each boy with a solemn expression. Tears brimmed her eyes. "What can I do to make you believe that?"

Like a shot, Nico bounced up and wrapped his plump arms around her neck. "*No llores,* Tití. *No llores.* Please don't cry. I love you. We know you love us."

Javi didn't move. He couldn't. He felt so confused. When his aunt had first started her tirade, he had felt angry. How could she continue to blame one of them—most likely him—for the water disturbances? She had already suspected him of being responsible for the chair and plate crashing against the wall the night of their spaghetti dinner. Would she soon start thinking he had something to do with the electrical disturbances?

But today's incidents were a bit different. In a way, he couldn't entirely blame her for suspecting them of playing with the water. It would have been possible for either Nico or him to sneak into the bathroom and kitchen, turn on the faucets, and leave them running. She was right that there were only three *people* in the house. Since she still wasn't convinced that a paranormal force could be responsible for the strange occurrences, it was only logical for her to suspect one of her nephews.

So, Javi decided, he couldn't be terribly angry at her for that. But the thing that really had him confused was that, despite the fact that she had warned them not to play with the water, and despite the fact that she thought one of them had deliberately disobeyed her and turned on the faucets, she still loved them.

She didn't *have* to love them. She might feel obligated to take them in and care for them, but she didn't have to love them.

Watching her hugging Nico, tears streaming down her cheeks, Javi had no doubt she loved them. And at that moment, he loved her, too. More than *he* had ever thought possible.

And so when Amparo looked up and held out an arm for him to come to her, he went.

25

"HEY, JAVA MAN AND WEEPING WILLOW. Wait up!"

Willo and Javi had ridden their bikes to the library for the second group meeting. As they finished locking up the bikes, Robert sauntered up the sidewalk with Max, the Cue Ball, at his side.

Willo crossed her eyes and shook her head. "Ignore them."

Robert's round face was redder than before. Javi noticed how his eyes seemed to bulge and his nose pointed up, prominently displaying his nostrils. He reminded Javi of Porky Pig. Javi turned away.

"I'm looking, but I don't see no cardinal on your head. Did he fly away?" Robert and Max snorted at his little joke. "I've heard of people wearing birds on their shoulders, but not on their heads. Aren't you afraid it'll poop in your hair?"

Javi clenched his jaw. His eyes narrowed.

"Ignore that lobotomized freak, Javi." Willo took his arm and tried to pull him away. He jerked his arm back and stood his ground.

"You know what, Maxie?" Robert turned to Max. "Maybe the Java Man wasn't talking about the birdie. Maybe he thinks he's a holy cardinal. Maybe he was going to wear his cardinal's hat today."

Max snickered and wagged his head in amusement.

Robert turned back to Javi. "Max, I think we should show more respect." Robert bowed his head. "May I kneel and kiss your ring, Your Holiness?"

Through clenched teeth, Javi replied, "You may kneel and kiss my—"

"Javi!" Willo yanked his arm hard. "It's late, let's go!"

Javi turned his back on Robert and Max and went inside with Willo. Giggling and snickering, the other boys followed.

Kimberly and Amy were already in the room when the others walked in. Ms. Watkins was sitting on a table in the front, legs crossed, wearing a hot-pink jumpsuit with a green silk scarf tied around her neck. Red curls spilled down her shoulders.

"Willo, so nice to see you today. How's your dad?"

"Fine, thanks," Willo muttered, taking her seat at the back.

"Wonderful, lovely! Javi, boys, please take your seats quickly. We've got a lot to get to today, and I want to discuss your first books."

Javi slumped down beside Willo. Robert and Max took their old seats, behind the girls, but Robert kept glancing back at Javi and smirking.

Ms. Watkins began again, "I've taken a look at my notes on all your comments from our last meeting. And I've made up a list of your likes and dislikes. I'll continue to assign books to each of you based on your comments, but remember, I also want you to swap books so that more than one of you critiques each book.

"Javi, since you didn't say much last time, I chose some more books for you. I thought you might enjoy books with multicultural themes, like the last book I gave you. I also thought we could all read them so we could discuss the issues that face people of color like Javi."

Javi's body tensed. His spine grew as straight as the two pillars at the front of the room. The phrase *gente de color* filled his mind. For the moment, he forgot his shyness in speaking English before strangers.

"What did you call me?" He enunciated each word so there could be no mistaking what he was saying.

Ms. Watkins looked up from her list. "I'm sorry, Javi, did you say something?"

"What did you call me?"

"I—I only said 'people of color'—"

"Why do you call me that?"

"I didn't mean to say anything offensive. I thought that was the politically correct term for minorities these days."

"I do not know about politically correct. I only know that you continue to try to make me something I am not. Why do you call me a colored person?"

Ms. Watkins's eyes, encircled with mascara-caked lashes, opened wide. "Oh no, no, I did not mean—I said *'person of color,'* not 'colored person.'"

Javi stood, facing Ms. Watkins. He looked directly into her eyes as he spoke. "I may not speak English very well, but I am not stupid. 'People of color' and 'colored people' mean the same thing. We studied recent American history in my old school. If the blacks in the 1960s did not like to be called 'colored people,' why do you think people from my country would feel differently? If I were black or mestizo or anything else, I would be proud of who I was. I would be proud because I love my family. I love my parents, and I am who I am because of them. But I am white. That is what my parents were. Why do you keep trying to make me something else?"

"I was only trying to be politically correct—"

"Again you say 'politically correct.' What does this mean?"

"It means"—Ms. Watkins's voice squeaked—"trying to be sensitive to others different from ourselves, using the right words—"

"Using the right words? Saying 'people of color' but not 'colored people'? How do you know what words to use? Who tells you these words? Who makes them up?"

Ms. Watkins's mouth gaped. She blinked her mascaraed lashes at Javi. She closed her mouth and cleared her throat. "I—I don't know—"

"Perhaps if you thought of people as individuals, as persons, and not as words, you would not have to worry about being, as you say, sensitive. I am Javier Leál. I am a person. And I like to read mysteries and adventures, horror books, and history fiction. I decide what I read because of what I like, not because of my race or my country."

Ms. Watkins gulped. "Yes, of course. Mysteries, horror, historical fiction. We have plenty of each, I'm sure."

She jotted a few notes on her pad, and Javi sat down. Drops of sweat rolled down his back. His heart galloped as if he had just finished first in the hundred-meter race at a swim meet. He could feel the other kids' eyes on him, but he stared straight ahead at Ms. Watkins.

At that moment the lights flickered several times and went out. The entire library plunged into darkness. In the next few seconds, Amy and Kimberly shrieked, Robert and Max hooted, and Ms. Watkins screeched, "Quiet, children, quiet!"

Then the lights flashed back on, followed by the loud *whoosh* of the air conditioner. The only vent in the tiny conference room was located above Ms. Watkins's head. It poured hurricane-strength cold air over the woman, blowing her long, red curls about her face and flinging her papers around the room like dead leaves in a fall storm.

26

"JAVI, JAVI!"

The moment Javi came home from the library, Nico and Fidel pounced on him. Nico tugged Javi's arm, pulling him down the hall.

"The boxes came. Our toys are here!"

"They're here already?" That was the best news Javi had heard since Tití Luisa phoned to tell the boys she had packed and mailed their personal things. "Where?"

"Tití had the man carry them upstairs. She's helping me unpack my boxes."

Javi and Nico bounced upstairs, with Fidel yipping at their heels. Amparo was sitting on the floor of Nico's room, gently unwrapping each item and placing it beside her. She had emptied two boxes and was surrounded with Nico's toys, picture books, and knickknacks. Nico's room was already taking on the personality of his old room.

"*Hola,* Javi," she said, looking up. "I had the nice fellow put your boxes in your room. I started helping Nico unpack. You may help us, and I'll help you when I'm done, or you may start on your stuff right away."

Javi couldn't wait to get to work. "If it is all right, I would like to unpack by myself."

"Sure. Call if you need help. Need a utility knife?"

"I have Papi's old knife," he said, running to his room.

Javi pulled the Swiss Army knife from his pocket and cut open all the boxes. Then he closed the door and sat on the floor next to the largest box. He wanted to relish this experience alone. He wanted to slowly unwrap each item and study it and remember.

By dinnertime Javi had hooked up his computer, stacked his favorite books on the bookshelves, arranged his swimming trophies on separate shelves, and tacked up his paintings, framed sketches, and the certificates of merit he'd received for superior work in art. He pinned a few of his favorite items onto empty spots he'd left for them on his bulletin board—a tiny figure of Goofy that Mami had gotten him at Disney World, a few medals and ribbons he'd won swimming, photos of his old swim team, and one of him and his best friend, Julio.

Javi smiled, remembering his swim team and how much fun he used to have. He loved swimming and missed it.

He placed two framed photographs of his family on his nightstand. One showed his parents hugging each other and smiling into the camera, smiling at him, young and happy. The other was a family photo of the four of them at Disney World. It had been taken just last summer. The

Disney World trip was a family tradition: Every year, the last week of summer, his dad would take them to Disney World. Nico had a similar picture in his room.

Finally Javi carefully distributed all his knickknacks, model airplanes and antique cars, and a few stuffed animals around his room. For three glorious hours he was lost in the past.

When the last box was empty and Amparo called him down for dinner, the warm glow of living in the past faded, and he remembered where he was.

Taking a last glance at his room, Javi headed for the kitchen. In the hall he was met with the familiar aroma of rice and beans and sizzling *bistec,* marinated steak and onions. He took a deep breath, enjoying the delicious smell. Amparo's rice and beans had greatly improved over the past few weeks, and her *bistec* was almost as good as Mami's had been.

"Don't forget to make mine a little rare," he said as he walked in.

"I know, I know. I've already served Nico a little steak. Could you help him cut it before it gets cold? Yours will be done in a minute."

Javi cut up Nico's steak, then went to the fridge to get the salad and bottles of dressing. After he set the table, Javi took his place across from Nico. It occurred to him that helping in the kitchen wasn't as bad as he had first believed it would be. Lately it had become almost second nature. He rarely gave it much thought anymore.

Another pleasant change was that Nico had been forbidden to bring Hamish to the table at mealtimes. Javi became so upset when he thought Hamish was at the table that Amparo finally agreed to reach a compromise. She explained to Nico that mealtime was "family time" and that Hamish, although a very good friend, was not really family. Nico could play with Hamish around the house, but not at mealtimes. (Amparo was still convinced that Hamish was a harmless imaginary friend.) When Nico began to whimper, she had agreed that he could serve Hamish some cookies and milk after dinner, so he wouldn't go hungry.

"How was your reading group today?" Amparo asked as she served Javi some thin steak fillets.

Javi pushed his rice and beans away from the steak. "Not good. I do not wish to return."

"What happened?"

As Amparo helped herself to rice, beans, and steak, Javi told her about Ms. Watkins's latest and what he had said to her. He went on to tell her about his run-ins with Robert. He hadn't yet told her about the cardinal-on-the-head incident from the first meeting, so he related that part first. Then he told her how Robert had teased him before class today, and how Willo insisted Javi ignore him.

"Willo is right. This Robert sounds like a very silly boy who is looking for attention, and it is best to ignore him."

"You do not understand. How do you ignore someone who makes fun of you?"

"I know it's difficult. But there are bullies in every part of the world, no matter how old you are. I've even had bosses and professors who were bullies. You can't avoid them by running away, because wherever you run, there's just another one waiting. Dealing with bullies never gets any easier. But you have to learn to stand up to them or hold your head high and walk away. The way you stood up to Ms. Watkins."

"That is easy for you to say. No one makes fun of your English."

"And someday, not so far in the future, no one will make fun of yours. You are learning very quickly. And this summer reading program should help. That's another good reason to stick with it."

Javi sighed. His aunt always had the answers. To her everything was logical. Everything had a way of working itself out. The way she explained it, everything seemed simple. But as much as he wanted to see things as she did, he could not. To him life was complicated, unpredictable, and frightening. Since his parents died, each morning had brought him face-to-face with a terrifying unknown world.

Amparo stood and stepped to the pantry. As she walked, her chair rocked back and forth, wobble-walking behind her. At first, she didn't notice, but when she spun around, bottle of Evian in her hand, she almost tripped over the chair.

"What—? Who put this chair here?"

Nico giggled. "The chair followed you, Tití."

"*Uh-huh.* The chair followed me. Okay, let's see if it follows me back."

As she slowly walked back to the table, the chair hobbled behind her.

"Okay, kids. Very funny." She felt the air behind her, as if she were searching for something. "Where's the string? I know you've rigged something. How did you do this?"

While Amparo grabbed at the air, groping for the offending invisible string that was supposedly used to pull the chair, Javi whispered to Nico, "Tell Hamish to stop that. He's going to get us in trouble again."

"It's not Hamish," Nico whispered back.

Javi felt the tiny hairs on his arms rise. "Hamish is not here—making the chair move?"

Nico shook his head. "Tití said Hamish could not eat with us. He's in the living room, playing with Fidel."

"Then who is moving that chair?"

"Nobody. It is moving by itself."

Later that evening Javi and Nico watched TV in the living room while Amparo worked in her office. Javi stared at the screen but couldn't concentrate. His mind kept drifting back to the events of the day: Robert. Ms. Watkins. And as if he didn't have enough problems, it seemed that Hamish wasn't content to simply play quietly with Nico. All the recent disturbances and this evening's incident with the chair hobbling after Amparo proved that. What else could possibly happen?

It was hard to believe that less than two months ago, he had had no worries. He had everything he wanted, and he was safe. *Why did Mami and Papi have to die?* Javi thought as a lump began to form in his throat. *Why did they leave us?*

Suddenly the couch the boys were sitting on began to rock forward and back, almost dumping the boys onto the floor. The cats, who had been curled at one end of the couch, hissed and darted from the room.

An armchair that sat to the right of the couch spun around and toppled over. Fidel pounced, barking and growling. The other armchair skated across the dark oak floor, entangling a throw rug around its legs and pulling it along in its wake. Fidel chased it, yipping and tugging at the rug with his teeth. But the chair kept sliding across the room, now pulling both the rug and Fidel.

The coffee table in front of the boys shimmied, rose about two feet in the air, flipped over, and fell back to the floor, legs pointing toward the heavens.

"Earthquake, Javi!" Nico cried, grabbing Javi's arm. "Let's run to the door like Tití taught us."

Fidel raced to the upturned table, growling and threatening to pounce.

"*Shh! Cállate,* Fidel, be quiet! Calm down, Nico." Javi pulled his arm away and turned to survey the damage. "It's not an earthquake. It's Hamish. Tell him to stop before Tití hears what's happening."

"No, Javi, it's not Hamish. Hamish is not here."

Javi's skin crawled just to think that something other than Hamish might be making the furniture move. But no. He didn't believe that. It had to be Hamish. Maybe he was watching them from the door. Or maybe he could make himself invisible to Nico just as he could to everyone else. And now that Javi and his aunt were starting to get along, this pesky little ghost was going to ruin things. If she saw the room the way it looked right now, she'd blame him for it.

"Help me, Nico." Javi ran around trying to set things right before Amparo came out to check on them. "We don't want Tití to see this mess. And tell that Hamish to stop making trouble."

"It wasn't him, Javi. I promise. He wasn't here."

Javi didn't want to frighten Nico by telling him that Hamish was a ghost and that ghosts could make themselves invisible and make things move about as if they were moving by themselves. Apparently Nico could see Hamish and accepted him as a little boy just like himself.

"Well," Javi said, "maybe Hamish was hiding so we

couldn't see him. I don't know—I just know he'd better stop making trouble."

"Creepers! Sounds like things are getting worse."

After an hour without further disturbances, Javi had called Willo and told her about the furniture moving around and about the water disturbances of the day before. He had been so concerned about the reading group that morning that he'd forgotten to tell her about the faucets and sprinklers turning on by themselves.

"Yes, very much worse. Have you read the books on the paranormal yet?" Javi asked.

"Just started to. And from what you've been telling me, I think I know what's going on."

"You do? Tell me, please."

"I'll come by tomorrow and explain it all, but it looks like you guys have more than just an ordinary ghost. Looks like you have a poltergeist."

AFTER HE FINISHED TALKING TO WILLO, Javi helped Nico into bed. Because it was the only way Nico would go to sleep, Javi played the nightly nursery-rhyme game their father used to play with him.

Kneeling beside Nico, Javi began:

> *Once there was a cat*
> *with feet made of rags,*
> *and his head was upside down.*
> *Want me to tell it again?*

Nico usually giggled and shrieked, *"¡Sí, sí, otra vez!"* But that night, he just smiled and nodded.

"Okay, one more time." Javi made his voice deep and serious.

*Once there was a cat
with feet made of rags,
and he had a paper tail.
Want me to tell it again?*

Nico gazed up sleepily. He gave a tiny nod.

Javi stroked his brother's hair as he watched the little boy's eyes struggle to stay open. He leaned over and kissed him on the forehead. "That's enough for tonight, *chico. Colorín colorado, este cuento se ha acabado.* I'll get Tití to come kiss you good night, *hmm?*"

Nico nodded.

Javi went downstairs to get his aunt. The door to her office was open a crack, and he could hear her murmuring. Something about the way she was talking made him stand still and listen. She was speaking softly in Spanish, probably to Tití Luisa. Javi stepped closer to the door.

"I just don't know," she was saying. "Nico seems to be adjusting nicely, under the circumstances. The younger they are, it seems, the more resilient. And he has that imaginary friend of his to keep him occupied. But"—she paused—"as much good as this imaginary friend is doing for Nico, it seems to be doing just the opposite for Javi. He gets sullen and often angry when Nico mentions or plays with his friend.

"Javi is convinced that—well, I won't burden you with the details. Javi is simply reacting abnormally to this imaginary friend of Nico's. Although it is normal for a boy Javi's age to be angry and frustrated with the changes he's had to make, and dealing with the pain of his parents' death, he doesn't seem to be adapting as well as Nico. He seems to be displacing his anger and frustrations, channeling them all toward Nico's imaginary friend, claiming that he's a threat and a danger to Nico."

Amparo paused a few minutes to listen, then replied, "No, I don't think he's dangerous. I don't see how. But Javi insists, and when I try to come up with logical explanations for the things he claims, we get into arguments. He accuses me of not believing, of not caring . . .

"He's even been doing some things around the house, playing tricks—then blaming them on this Hamish. So far, nothing dangerous, but I just don't know . . . I'm doing all I can to reach him. I thought things were getting better, but at dinner tonight, he tried another trick. I don't know how he does them. They're as good as a professional magician's tricks. I—I found a book in his room once. Maybe he's getting these ideas from books, then staging things to look like . . . Oh, I don't know! He's such a bright boy, and bright children learn quickly. I'm afraid . . . Luisa, I think I'm going to have him talk to a therapist friend of mine—before things get worse. He's a child psychologist, and very good . . ."

Javi stopped listening. It was even worse than he had suspected. His aunt not only thought he was responsible for the strange disturbances in the house, but if she wanted him to see a child psychologist, didn't that mean she also thought he was crazy?

The next morning Willo called to say she wouldn't be able to come by after all. Her grandmother was sick, and Willo and her father would be spending the day with her. But she promised to come by the following day, if possible.

Amparo had left Javi to look after Nico for a couple of hours while she ran some errands in town. She'd invited them along, but thinking that Willo was coming over, Javi asked her to let him baby-sit. As usual Amparo took her cell phone, instructing Javi to call if necessary, and promised she'd never be more than ten minutes away.

Javi watched through the kitchen window as she drove off, remembering the conversation he had overheard last night before going to bed.

Rage bubbled inside him. Why couldn't she just believe him? Better yet, why couldn't Hamish just leave them alone? Then Javi wouldn't have to worry about convincing his aunt that Hamish wasn't imaginary, that he was really a ghost. Things would begin to settle down, and they might have a chance at becoming a family. It would never be the same as the family he and Nico had with Mami and Papi, but he so longed for the safety and stability of a family again. And he knew that Amparo wanted that, too.

Then another thought occurred to him. Maybe the problems he was having with his aunt were partly his own fault. If he had stopped trying to convince Amparo that the house was haunted, she never would have thought he was crazy. He should have tried to figure out by himself what to do with Hamish. Now everything that Hamish did would be blamed on him. If only he hadn't pushed . . .

A clattering noise near the stairs made Javi spin around. Another noise made him stiffen and stand still, listening. He heard it again. The slow, deliberate *thump, thump, thump* of someone descending the stairs.

But Nico was on the front lawn, playing with Fidel. There was no one else in the house, was there?

Javi tiptoed to the hall door and peeked out. As far as he could tell, no one was on the stairs, but the thumping continued. Javi took a deep breath and ventured into the hall, tiptoeing along until he was directly facing the stairs. He stifled a gasp.

Two large pans were marching down the staircase, each hitting one step after the other as if an unseen person were wearing the pans as shoes, one on each foot. *Thump, thump, thump,* they marched down the steps . . . toward him.

Distracted by the marching pans, Javi didn't immediately notice the assortment of cookware that had congregated at the top of the stairs. It was as if all the pots and pans had been spirited from the kitchen and assembled on the carpet of the second floor.

A clattering noise, like the one he had first heard, made him look up in time to see the pots and pans lift from the carpet, clanging and clattering as they bumped against each other, and begin to float down toward him. At first they seemed to glide gently, then they picked up incredible speed and shot at him like flying saucers. Javi jumped away, falling onto the floor in the living room, and barely missed getting clobbered by the flying cookware, which fell with a deafening crash at the bottom of the stairs.

The two pots that had been marching down the stairs finally reached the last step and jumped with a *clang* onto the pile with the others.

Javi stared at the heap of shining copper and aluminum that now lay lifeless. The pots and pans had attacked him! He was sure of it. If he hadn't jumped away when he had, they would have hit him.

Hamish!

It had to be.

Javi ran back to the kitchen, giving the pile of pots and pans a wide berth, and looked out the window. Nico was on the front lawn, throwing a large beach ball at someone across the lawn who was throwing it back. When Javi looked to see who could be playing with Nico, he saw no one. The ball seemed to hit an invisible wall and fly back on its own.

If Hamish was outside playing with Nico, who could—?

Javi shook his head. What was happening? If the evil thing couldn't enter their house, as Hamish claimed, and Hamish wasn't behind these attacks, then who was?

Whatever the answer, one thing seemed certain: This new force was attacking Javi.

"SO HAS ANYTHING NEW HAPPENED since the last time we talked?" Willo asked Javi the next morning, spreading the library books in front of her.

She was curled up on his bed with ZsaZsa and Misifú, who had followed her into the room. Javi couldn't help noticing how much Willo reminded him of a cat. She seemed to have a knack for settling into comfortable positions.

"Very much has happened," Javi replied. Remembering Ms. Watkin's comment about good news and bad news, he said, "Would you like to hear the bad news or the much more bad news?"

"Crackers! I've only been gone one day. What else happened?"

"Tití Amparo wants to send me to a therapist—a child psychologist—and there appears to be a third ghost."

Willo's eyes, dark blue today to match her navy blue U.C. Berkeley sweatshirt, opened wide. She sat up and curled her legs under her. ZsaZsa stepped daintily onto her lap and tramped around until she had found a comfortable spot in which to curl up. Misifú stayed where she was, next to Willo, and blinked with disdain at having had her nap disrupted.

"A therapist? A third ghost? Hurry up and tell me what happened."

Javi began his story with Amparo's telephone call to Luisa and how he overheard her say that she was considering sending him to a therapist. Then he told Willo about the pots-and-pans attack and how he had barely finished putting them away before Amparo got home.

"Crickets!" Willo said. "You did have quite a day."

Javi glanced at Willo. "What do the books say? The other night you said we might have a polter-something?"

"Poltergeist." Willo picked up one of her books and read a line. "It's 'a paranormal phenomenon that manifests itself by rappings, noises, and creating disorder.'"

Javi considered this. "'Creating disorder.' Yes, that is Hamish."

"No, that is definitely *not* Hamish. A poltergeist is always invisible. Although Hamish is usually invisible to you, Nico seems to see him, and you have seen him in a mirror. I'll tell you about Hamish and mirrors in a minute, but first the poltergeist."

"Then you do believe that there is another ghost in the house—in addition to Hamish."

"Another force, yes. And I think it was this force that caused the playful disturbances you've told me about and yesterday's attack on you—not Hamish. See, according to these books, a poltergeist isn't really a ghost. Not the way we think of ghosts—not the spirit or soul of a dead person."

Javi felt a chill settle over him. Something about the way Willo was looking at him made him feel apprehensive. "Not a ghost? Then what?" he asked, not really wanting to know.

"Well, there are two distinctive traits that distinguish a poltergeist from an apparition or a ghost. First, poltergeist activities almost always occur in a house in which a child lives. Second, these disturbances tend to be naughty, playful types of acts, usually harmless. But they have been known to become more dangerous."

"The pots and pans could have hurt me if I had not jumped away."

"Yes, and there is something interesting about yesterday's attack. Was that the first time you were directly attacked?"

Javi nodded.

"I thought so." Willo lifted ZsaZsa off her lap and leaned toward Javi, an intense look in her eyes. "I'm going to tell you what the parapsychologists believe causes a poltergeist, but you have to promise to stay calm."

"*Muy bien,* yes. I shall stay calm."

"Researchers think that most poltergeist activity is caused by recurrent, spontaneous psychokinesis—"

"Wait! You are using those large words again."

"Sorry. Psychokinesis is when items are moved by the use of the human mind."

Javi shifted uncomfortably in his seat. "What are you saying?"

"Let me finish. Parapsychologists believe that at least ninety percent of poltergeist activity occurs when a frustrated teen or preadolescent is around. They think the child or teenager releases uncontrolled surges of psycho-kinesis when he or she is angry, upset, or disturbed. With their minds, these kids can make things move or fly about as if an unseen hand is moving them."

Javi stared at Willo in disbelief. "The child? Me? Are you saying *I* am doing these things? You believe like Tití Amparo—"

"No, Javi, I don't think like Amparo, that you're playing tricks on purpose. But it's possible that, with your mind, you're doing these things and aren't aware of it."

"No! It cannot be!"

"Javi, you promised to stay calm. Let me explain, please. You wanted me to help you find out what's happening. Do you still want to know?"

Javi crossed his arms over his chest. He couldn't believe that Willo could betray him like this. He glared at her. His chest heaved; his nostrils flared. As Javi stared, angry thoughts tumbling about his mind, the floor began to shake. Items on the walls rattled. The plastic model airplanes on Javi's shelves rose up in the air, assumed a V formation, and dove at him. A wing scratched his face; a wheel nicked his ear. Javi ducked, but the planes continued to attack.

He fell to the ground, arms over his head. "Stop, stop! Leave me alone!"

Three of the planes collapsed unharmed on his bed. Two others hit the floor: One glided onto the thick throw rug, but the other crashed into the wood floor. Its wing and propeller snapped with the impact.

Javi glanced around. Everything else appeared to be back to normal. He looked up at Willo.

She let out her breath. "Now will you listen?"

29

JAVI SAT BACK IN HIS CHAIR. His shoulders slumped. He felt defeated.

"I will listen," he said.

Willo scooted to the edge of the bed. "Okay, here's what I think is happening. You've had a difficult time these past two months. You lost your parents, you had to leave your home to come to a new country to live with an aunt you hardly knew, you have to speak a new language, you have to do things you don't want to do. See what I'm getting at?"

"No, I do not. I know all of these things. But what do they have to do with what is happening here—and with the ghosts?"

"The ghosts are a different matter. We'll talk about them later. Your biggest problem right now is getting rid of the poltergeist activity so things between you and Amparo can improve, right?"

Javi nodded.

Willo continued, "Let me ask you some questions. Do these strange disturbances ever take place when you're not in or near the house?"

Javi thought about that. "I suppose they do not. Tití has never complained about anything strange that happened when I am not here."

"Okay. Think carefully about the times when the disturbances took place. What were you thinking or feeling just before they happened?"

Javi tried to remember. He thought back to the first "earthquake," on the afternoon they came to live with Amparo. It happened in the room he was to share with Nico—the dark, tiny space shared with Amparo's storage boxes. He had felt abandoned by his parents and unwanted by his aunt. The next "earthquake" occurred when he was yelling at Nico to get rid of Hamish. Then, on the night of the spaghetti dinner, when the chair and plate smashed against the wall, he was angry with Hamish. As he recalled each occurrence, he remembered that it had been preceded by his feeling angry, lost, unwanted, and frustrated.

Javi looked at Willo. "I remember. I was angry—very angry."

Willo smiled sympathetically. "And what about yesterday—before the pots and pans attacked you? Who were you angry at?"

Javi knew what she was getting at. He had been blaming himself for continuing to try to convince Amparo that the house was haunted.

"I was angry at myself," he replied. Then something occurred to him. "But I still do not understand. Many people are angry and frustrated. Why do they not make things move with their minds?"

"That's one of the things the researchers don't understand yet. Maybe only certain people who have strong psychic abilities can cause poltergeist activities. Remember, you've had some clairvoyant episodes. You dreamed about your parents' accident before it happened."

Javi nodded. "And other things. I have felt other things that came true." He told her of his nightmare about Nico lost in the woods, and how a few weeks later, he woke up sensing something was wrong on the morning Nico ran into the woods. "But what do I do now? How can I control this psycho—what is it called?"

"Psychokinesis. I don't know if you can. What you have is called recurrent, spontaneous psychokinesis because it just happens spontaneously—that means without being planned. And it's recurrent because it happens more than once and may continue to happen for a while. But there is some good news."

"Ah," said Javi with a wry smile, "you gave me the bad news first."

Willo grinned. "The good news is that poltergeist activity rarely lasts long. A few weeks, maybe a couple of months—"

"A couple of months! Tití will have me put away in a *manicomio* if this continues."

"A what?"

"A place for crazy people."

"Cripes, an insane asylum?" Willo gave a loud snort. "No, she won't. Amparo loves you, you must know that. I've seen how close you guys have grown lately. Anyway, maybe now that you know you might be causing these weird things, you can try to control your anger. That might help stop the poltergeist activities. And"—Willo picked up one of the books—"there's something else."

"Good news or bad news?"

"A little of both. Depends on how you look at it. This book says that since these poltergeist kids are upset and frustrated, talking to a therapist helps."

"Now you think like Tití Amparo, that I am crazy!"

"Shh-hh!" Willo gestured with her hands for Javi to calm down. She glanced nervously at the bookshelves and the items on the walls. "You don't have to be crazy to go to a therapist. Just confused or upset. Talking helps. The therapist can show you how to work through your problems, not just react to them. A therapist might help you figure out a way to release your anger that isn't quite so . . . violent."

"How do you know so much about therapy?"

"After Mom died, I was like you. Angry, feeling abandoned. Daddy took me to a friend of Amparo's. I didn't have to go long. It did help."

"Perhaps." Javi shrugged. He didn't want to think about the therapist anymore. "What about Hamish and the evil ghost? Are they my fault, too?"

"I've been thinking about that. See, parapsychologists haven't found much to prove the existence of ghosts or spirits. A few cases can't be explained any other way. But *this* book says"—Willo picked up another book—"that most apparitions may be created by the human mind.

"It's too hard to explain all the theories, but basically an area—like the woods—may be 'haunted' because something very tragic or emotional happened there. The area around it picks up the psychic energy released by the people who died or suffered there—it's called 'psychometry' or 'place memory.' Everyone has psychic energy, and it intensifies under times of stress."

Willo glanced at Javi in that knowing way she had. He felt the chill begin to descend on him once more.

"That psychic energy, or place memory," Willo went on, "remains in the surrounding trees, rocks, and structures for years, even centuries, and can be picked up by someone who is sensitive to paranormal phenomena."

"Like me," Javi said bleakly.

Willo nodded. "That's why you sensed the evil ghost's presence and sensed that Hamish was not simply an imaginary friend."

"But what about Nico? Why does he see Hamish?"

"There may be a combination of factors going on there." She curled up on the bed. "Little kids are more sensitive to the paranormal, then they tend to outgrow it. So maybe Nico can see and hear ghosts, while older people can't. Or maybe you are transmitting Hamish's image to Nico."

"How?"

"Maybe you sense him and are causing his image to appear to Nico by telepathy or by some other psychic phenomenon. Or maybe Hamish is simply one of those unexplained, honest-to-goodness ghosts, and Nico's presence brings him out. They're about the same age, and Hamish may be lonely."

"Why can Nico see Hamish and I cannot?"

Willo shook her head. "Who knows? But you did see him in the mirror, and I read about mirrors. In some reported cases, people have glanced in a mirror and seen the image of someone who has died—the way you did. So maybe, in this case, you can see Hamish only in a mirror."

Javi gave a frustrated sigh. There was so much to think about. So much confusing information. How could he sort it all out? Instead of making him feel better, Willo's information made him feel worse. More than ever, in the pit of his stomach, he felt the weight of impending doom.

"Willo, if my poltergeist goes away in a few weeks, will Hamish and the evil one go away, too?"

Willo shrugged. "I really don't know, Javi."

Javi rose and stepped to the window. He gazed out at the footbridge and the woods beyond. A tiny shiver slithered up his back.

"Then I shall have to find a way to make them leave on my own," he said. "Because if I do not rid our family of the ghosts, I know something will happen—something very bad."

30

"HEY, IF IT ISN'T THE WILL-O'-THE-WISP, hanging out with the Cardinal."

Javi and Willo, who had been walking Fidel along the driveway, snapped their heads around. Red-faced Robert straddled his bike at the end of the driveway. When they turned, he seemed to take it as an invitation to approach.

Willo thrust her fists onto her hips. "What are you doing here, Robert?"

"That's not a very neighborly attitude."

"We aren't your neighbors."

"Well, it's not a very nice way to treat a guest."

"You're certainly no guest."

"I didn't come to visit you, anyway." Robert's gaze slid to Javi. "This is where you live, isn't it, Java Man?"

Javi's eyes narrowed. He could feel his pulse quicken, throbbing in his ears. "What do you want?"

"To exchange books."

Willo stepped forward. "You should have called."

"Why? Because I caught you guys in a little lovers' tryst?"

Willo gave an exasperated groan. "You're—you're . . . such a *moron*!"

Javi's ears and neck burned. He glanced at Willo. Her face had blushed crimson under her tan.

Robert's face split into a wide, ugly smirk. "So I was right. You two have a little thing going on."

Javi clenched his jaw and squeezed his fists into tight balls. "This is private property. You are not welcome. Please leave."

Robert jumped off his bike and leaned it against a tree. "But that's not fair. Then I can't exchange books with you."

"I do not wish to exchange with you. I shall choose someone else with whom to exchange."

"*Oo-oo*, hoity-toity. You shall, shall you? And who shall you choose, your little love blossom, the weeping tree?"

Javi's chest heaved. "I told you to go away!"

The sound of metal scraping made Robert swing around. His bicycle had slid down the side of the tree and collapsed on the gravel.

"Come on, Javi," Willo said, placing a calming hand on his shoulder, "let's take Fidel inside."

As Robert scrambled back to set his bike upright, Javi and Willo led the little dog back to the house.

Javi handed Willo the leash. "Please take Fidel inside. I will be in soon."

"I'll take him in, but I'll be right back," she replied.

When Willo stepped inside, Javi turned to Robert, who had walked up behind him. "I told you to go away."

Another smirk twisted the boy's face. "Why? You gonna go smooch with the Willowy One?"

Javi glanced at the house. His eyes met Willo's as she watched from the kitchen window. Like a branch breaking under too much strain, he felt something snap inside him. Everything seemed to blur and speed to a dizzying rate—a video on fast-forward. He heard the growl of an animal, so close it seemed inside him. Grabbing the front of Robert's sweatshirt, he pulled the boy toward him.

"I told you to leave!" he screamed in Robert's round face, then let him go.

Robert backed away. He looked stunned at first, then the ugly smirk returned. "You really have the hots for her, don't you?"

Javi stepped forward, thrusting his arms toward Robert's chest. At that very moment, the door slammed and Willo screamed, "Javi, stop!"

Startled by her voice, he pulled back so that his fingertips barely touched Robert. Yet Robert flew back in a high arc, arms and legs flailing. He landed on the lawn and continued to skid backward on his rump as if he were on a water slide. Then he crashed spread-eagled into the hedges that bordered the lawn.

As Robert stared at Javi, open mouthed, the hose near the house began to uncoil and slither toward him. At his feet, the hose slowly rose before him like a hypnotized cobra, pointing its nozzle at his chest. Robert, in turn, stared, mesmerized. Suddenly water exploded from the nozzle.

"*Ah-hhh!*" Robert screamed and slapped the hose away from him. But the hose was alive, snapping whiplike and wriggling and spraying. Robert struggled to his feet. With the hose in close pursuit, he ran—slipping, sliding, and howling—across the wet grass.

Giving Javi one last glance, Robert blew by him and scrambled to his bike, barely waiting to get on before pumping away.

The look he had given Javi was one of pure terror.

When Willo flew down the front steps to Javi's side, he was still shaking. His chest was heaving, and he felt light-headed and dizzy. He could barely remember what had just happened. It was as if he were awaking from a disturbing dream.

Through a cottonlike haze, he heard Willo's voice. It sounded distant, muffled. He tried to make out the words.

". . . you okay? Come inside." Willo took his arm and led him up the front steps and into the house.

His legs felt rubbery, but they held. He followed her upstairs to his room. The day had darkened, and his room was full of shadows. Outside the window, black rain clouds tumbled over each other as if in a race to be the first to leave the ocean and burst open on inland valleys.

"I must do something, Willo," Javi said, sinking onto his bed. "This cannot continue. I have no control . . ."

Willo sat beside him. "Do you want to tell Amparo?"

Javi shook his head. "How can I tell her? What can I tell her that she will believe?"

"I wish I could help."

"You have done very much already. At least I know what is causing these terrible things—me. Did you see what I did to Robert?"

Willo chuckled. "I've never seen him run so fast."

"But I might have hurt him badly. I did not want to

hurt him. I only wanted him to leave—to stop bothering us. But I was so angry. He said mean things. Then . . . I cannot remember what happened."

"Well, you don't have to worry about Robert anymore. I don't think he'll bother you again."

"But I have to worry about other things. Hamish and"— Javi glanced out the window and pointed with his chin— "that one. The wicked thing that waits in the woods. What if something should happen to Nico because of them? Or even to Tití Amparo, who suspects nothing? What if she goes out to the woods and that thing harms her?"

"Amparo has lived here for years. The ghosts have never chosen to harm her before."

"They may not have had a reason before. Now that I am here, they may have one. You said so yourself. I may be the one causing them to appear."

"Oh." Willo scooted back against the wall. "You may be right."

"So what can I do?"

Willo was silent for a few minutes, biting her lower lip as she thought. "Stresses. You have to find a way to relieve your stresses and frustrations and some way to work out your aggressions—your anger."

"Are you speaking of the therapist?"

"Yes, talking to a therapist would be a start. Getting away from the house more might help, too. When school starts, that will get you out of the house."

Javi groaned. "I do not wish to discuss school. I believe it will add to my problems. Anyway, I must learn to control my psychokinesis before school starts."

Willo giggled. "You're right, I forgot. We can't have kids and equipment flying around the school."

"I wish I could laugh about this as you do," he said with a trace of a smile. "Perhaps I can try to learn from you. You laugh a great deal."

"You *are* pretty intense. A little lightening up wouldn't hurt."

He nodded. "I shall try. And maybe I can begin swimming again. I miss swimming."

"I noticed your trophies," said Willo, glancing at his shelves. "You must be pretty good."

"Papi taught Nico and me to swim when we were babies. Sometimes I feel like a fish. I enjoy the water."

"Why don't you have Amparo enroll you in the city swim team?"

"I do not know . . ." Javi hesitated, not wanting to admit the real reason.

Willo seemed to read his mind. "Is it that you don't want to meet new kids?"

Javi shrugged.

"Oh, crackers, Javi. You shouldn't be embarrassed about your English. You're doing really great. And you've improved a lot in the last few weeks. Pretty soon you can start concentrating on teaching me Spanish. *¿Qué dices, chico?*"

Javi managed a grin. "Perhaps, but I say stupid things sometimes."

"We all say stupid things sometimes. It's no reason to isolate yourself from other people or to keep from doing things you love."

Javi reflected on Willo's words, knowing she was right. What kind of life could he possibly have if all he ever did was hide out at the house? If only everyone were as understanding as Willo.

Javi sighed. "Perhaps you are right."

"Good. So what do we have?" Willo began to count on her fingers. "First you'll ask Amparo if you can start some therapy with her friend. Then you'll start swimming. I can show you where the city pool is, and you can start swimming laps on your own. Maybe I'll even join you sometimes. That'll get you out of the house and help you work out your aggressions."

Javi stepped to the window. A streak of lightning split the dark sky above the gnarled oaks, and the windows shuddered with the roar of thunder.

"But the most important," he said, staring at the old oak near the wooden bridge, "I must find a way to rid the house and the woods of the ghosts."

IT SEEMED AS IF A FAUCET had been turned on in the heavens; rain poured in heavy sheets. The wind had picked up speed and blew the sheets of rain almost horizontally against the wooden house.

Since Amparo's house had no attic, Javi could hear the steady tattoo of rain beating on the roof directly through the ceiling of his room. The sound seemed to soothe his frazzled nerves, and he was able to concentrate deeply. He escaped into his new book from Ms. Watkins—a page-turner of a mystery, this time—and forgot his problems for a while.

On the afternoon of the third day of nonstop rain, Javi heard Nico whimpering. He set down his book and peeked into Nico's room. Nico had crawled under the bed; only the bottoms of his Nikes were visible.

"Hamish!" he wailed. "Where are you? Please come out."

178

"Nico, what's wrong?"

Nico crawled out from under the bed. When he saw Javi, his eyes brimmed with tears. "It's Hamish. I cannot find him."

"Hamish is gone?" Javi asked hopefully.

Nico's lower lip trembled. He nodded.

Javi picked him up and sat the little boy on his lap. "Don't worry about Hamish, Nico. I'm sure he's just fine."

"No, Hamish was frightened. He doesn't like storms."

Javi remembered that little Hamish had disappeared during a bad storm. He shivered at the thought of a small child in a rainstorm in the woods, alone ... or worse, with a kidnapper.

He hugged Nico close.

What would he do if something like that happened to his little brother? It was unthinkable. Nothing like that could ever happen, could it?

"Maybe Hamish is hurt," Nico mumbled, bringing Javi back to reality.

"*Hmm?* No, I don't think so. He's probably hiding from the storm," Javi offered, hoping he was wrong and that Hamish had left them forever. "He'll be back when it's over."

Nico regarded him with trusting eyes. "Do you think so?"

"Sure, wait and see," Javi replied, feeling like a traitor for wanting otherwise. With all his heart he hoped they'd seen the last of Hamish and of the wicked thing in the woods.

Javi awoke sweating. His heart slapped his rib cage in rhythm to the branches scraping the side of the house. The wind moaned like a wounded animal, deep and haunting.

Something inside him wanted to howl with the wind, to cry out in pain. A penetrating sadness, a sense of something precious lost, consumed him.

It was the same feeling he'd had the morning of the day his parents were killed.

He must have been dreaming, but about what? There had been a storm, dark woods . . . Nico!

Javi raced to Nico's room.

The room was dark. It was just before five in the morning, but from the night-light in the hall, he could make out a small lump in the bed. He sighed with relief and stepped over to straighten the blankets.

"Nico?" he whispered.

Nico made no sound, and the lump in the bed did not budge.

Javi's stomach flopped over like a dead fish. Gingerly he touched the lump. It was squishy, not solid. In a panic, he mashed it down. Pillows. Nico had arranged two small pillows where he slept and covered them with the blanket.

Although Javi knew for certain that Nico was no longer in the house, he raced from room to room in his bare feet, careful not to awaken Amparo, and searched for his brother. As he had feared, there was no sign of Nico.

Javi returned to Nico's room. Nico's rain boots and slicker were gone. So was Pulito, the little stuffed dog.

Javi's gaze drifted to the window, to the dark, menacing woods, to the storm.

Nico was out there.

With the ghosts.

Javi's nightmare was coming true!

Javi threw on some warm clothes and carried his boots and slicker downstairs so he wouldn't disturb Amparo.

Nico probably hadn't been gone long, and if he was lucky, Javi could find him and be back before their aunt awoke.

He grabbed a heavy-duty flashlight from the den and looked for Amparo's cell phone in case he needed it. The phone wasn't where she usually left it. There was no more time. Making the sign of the cross, he slipped out the back door.

A thunderous roar seemed to come from the creek. Javi pointed his flashlight. The tiny babbling brook had turned into roaring whitewater rapids that slapped the bottom of the footbridge.

"*Dios mío,* Nico, where are you?" Javi muttered as he dashed for the bridge and darted across. He prayed that his brother had stayed away from the edge of the water and was wandering close by, in the woods.

A few yards from the bridge, on the path that Nico had taken before, Javi spotted something lying in the mud. Aiming his flashlight, he recognized the tan, fuzzy form, now drenched and covered with mud.

"Pulito!" he cried, pouncing on the scruffy stuffed dog. "Oh, Nico," he said, glancing around, "you *are* out here. You crazy little kid. Wait till I get my hands on you!"

Javi took shelter from the wind and rain between a cluster of heavy low oaks. He squeezed Pulito until all the water was wrung out, and with a handkerchief, he rubbed the mud off the shaggy fur.

"Nico, Nico, where are you?" He buried his face in the damp fur.

As he held the little stuffed dog against him, colors and images exploded in his head. Clutching the dog, he stared at the images as if he were watching a movie.

Nico, in his yellow slicker, waddled across the foot-bridge. The hood of his slicker concealed most of his face, but Javi could see the bill of his red cap peeking out above his eyes. Nico's head oscillated back and forth, his eyes scanned the woods, and his mouth opened as he called, "Hamish! Hamish! Where are you?"

Clutched to Nico's chest was Pulito.

At the edge of the bridge, Nico stopped. He stared straight ahead. Terror filled his eyes. His mouth opened, but no sound came out. He darted to the left, down the path, into the woods. He stumbled and fell. He dropped Pulito. Scrambling to his feet, he ran into the woods.

Only Nico's little stuffed dog remained, lying in the mud.

Javi blinked. The image was gone. But the feeling was not. He could still feel Nico's terror.

Nico had seen it.

The wicked thing.

The evil ghost was chasing Nico.

Javi crashed down the path that Nico had taken. Branches ripped their brittle fingers over his slicker, clawed at his face. The stuffed dog, tucked under his belt inside his slicker, banged against his thighs as he ran.

"Nico!" Javi yelled over the howling wind. "Nico! Where are you?"

He kept running, scanning the area with his flashlight. He had to find Nico—soon. If the evil one was after Nico, who knew what he might do to the little boy when he caught him? What did he want? Did he want to kidnap Nico and hold him hostage for some imaginary ransom? Was he trying to re-create the kidnapping of Hamish Brenden McTavish, trying to get it right?

Javi groaned. How could he have let this happen? He

should have guessed Nico might venture into the woods looking for Hamish. Nico had been so worried about Hamish. If only he'd paid more attention! The signs had been there last night. Nico had retreated inside himself, the way he had after their parents died—the way he had just before he met Hamish. Even their nightly ritual of playing "The Cat with Legs of Rags" hadn't cheered him up. He hadn't even wanted to play.

Oh, why didn't I pay more attention? Javi thought.

Javi stopped to catch his breath. He glanced around. The tiny path had disappeared, and he had no idea where he was or how far he'd gone. He checked the time. Half an hour had passed since he left the house. He didn't know how long Nico had been out in the storm.

"I should have told Tití," he said aloud. "If I had told her, she would have gotten the police to help us search. Now we're both lost, and Nico's with that . . . thing."

Javi's stomach sloshed. The grapefruit-sized lump in his throat throbbed. He was cold, wet, and terrified for Nico. If something horrible happened, it would be his fault.

So now it was up to him. Nico's life was in his hands.

Javi held Pulito again, trying to see more images of Nico. But all he accomplished was tapping into the horror that the little boy had felt when he fell and dropped the stuffed dog. If he wanted to know what had happened to Nico after he left Pulito, Javi would have to find an object that was near Nico *after* he dropped the little dog.

What had Willo told him about psychic energy released at times of great emotional stress? Didn't she say that the surrounding areas absorbed the energy? The trees, the rocks, the ground, maybe even the air.

Javi spread out his arms and turned slowly, trying to read anything in the air. He touched nearby bushes. He ran to an old twisted oak and, eyes closed, placed his hands on its trunk. He slid his hands down the trunk to the roots, then to the thick moss at its base.

Nothing.

He felt the soggy ground, digging his fingers into the mud.

Still nothing.

He stood. Rain continued to attack the earth with no hint of stopping.

This was not the right place. Nico had not been here. Javi felt it in his gut. Somehow Javi would have to find his way back to a spot where Nico had been and proceed from there.

This time he wouldn't run aimlessly. This time he would use his senses.

His psychic senses.

JAVI BEGAN TO TRACE his way back through the woods along the path he thought he'd taken. He hoped it was the right path. Everywhere he went, everything looked the same, heavy oaks, interlocking branches overhead, ferns and brambles cluttering the ground, tall pines here and there.

But Javi had ceased to look with his eyes. Now he was relying solely on inner sight. He walked slowly, touching, feeling, holding out his arms like a blind person.

At last Javi sensed something. He stopped. Closing his eyes, he spread out his arms and turned slowly in a circle. His heart began to pound. His legs trembled. Nausea tugged at the back of his throat.

Javi's eyes snapped open. A little boy in a yellow slicker ran toward him.

"Nico!" he cried, and held out his arms.

The little boy's face was a mask of horror. He glanced back as he ran. A dark, shimmering shadow hovered a few feet behind him. Nico ran toward Javi, screaming, as if he didn't see him.

"Nico, come here. It's me, Javi!"

Javi ran to the boy. As they met, Javi held out his arms to encircle his brother, but Nico ran through him as though Javi were made of mist.

"Nico!" Javi turned.

Nico stumbled and fell at the spot where Javi had been standing when he first saw him. The dark shadow descended upon the little boy. Javi pounced on them, but the image vanished.

"Nico-ooo!" Javi took on Nico's terror. The nausea grew worse. He fell to his knees, trembling, doubled over, and threw up.

Weak and shaky, he pushed himself up and moved on. He was on the right path now. He would find Nico, he was sure of it.

But would he be in time?

Moving more quickly now, Javi touched outstretched branches and felt tree trunks along the way to make sure he was on the right track. So long as the feeling of being hunted and afraid stayed with him, he knew Nico had traveled that path.

Nico's fear was different from his own, and Javi was able to distinguish them. Javi's fear was in his heart, deep and compelling. It was a fear for his brother's safety, a fear that he would be too late, a fear that kept him moving and searching and hoping with no thought for his own safety.

Nico's was a cold terror that Javi felt deep in the pit of

his stomach. It tugged at his throat and made him physically weak. He had to gather all the strength he could muster to keep touching things that would evoke the terror. But evoking the terror was necessary if he was to stay on the right path.

Running again, Javi stumbled on a rock and fell.

That was when he saw it. Nico's red cap. It was hooked to the branch of a low bush. Gingerly Javi picked up the cap and clutched it to his chest. He closed his eyes.

His heart began to pound, and a feeling of urgency overtook him. He opened his eyes.

Nico zipped past him, calling, "Hamish! Hamish, wait for me!"

The little boy darted behind a bush. Javi followed. Nico raced ahead, calling to Hamish and glancing back periodically. Javi glanced back, too, to see whether the evil ghost was still pursuing Nico.

He saw nothing but gnarled tree trunks with outstretched, beckoning limbs. The evil one had vanished. Even the sense of being hunted had been replaced by a sense of desperation, a need to reach something. Javi recognized this feeling as Nico's need to reach Hamish.

"Slow down, Hamish, I can't keep up!" Nico called, running and stumbling through the trees. "Come back, Hamish!"

Javi realized that something else had changed. Now, instead of the evil one chasing Nico, Hamish seemed to be leading Nico farther and farther into the woods.

Were the ghosts working together? Or was little Hamish simply running from the evil one as Nico had been?

Before Javi could give the matter more thought, Nico

ran into a small clearing covered with waist-high grass and bushes. The surrounding trees kept pockets of violent wind swells contained in the clearing, creating miniature funnel clouds that howled and whipped sheets of rain into icy swirls. The grass undulated in oceanlike waves.

Javi was pushing through the wind and grass, trying to catch up, when he saw Nico stop. The hood of Nico's slicker blew back, exposing his red cap and a frozen scream.

From the depths of the ground rose the dark, shimmering shadow of the evil ghost. It hovered for a moment, and in that moment Javi managed to reach his brother. Javi lunged toward Nico, grabbing for his shoulders, but his hands grasped only pellets of swirling rain.

As the shadow descended, enveloping Nico, Javi felt a cold more intense than he'd felt in his life. It was a hard cold that penetrated his bones, making them feel achy and brittle. A funnel cloud surrounded Javi, whipping the rain against his face, flattening the weeds and grass, and exposing a wall of wooden planks at his feet. The wall tilted toward him at an angle and was spotted with moss and lichen. A long, heavy tree trunk that had apparently broken from its stump years before stretched across the wooden planks.

Lightning cracked overhead. A low groan and a rumbling shook his feet. The dead trunk rolled toward him and fell off the wooden wall. Javi jumped, but the log rolled through his legs as if they weren't there. With a creak and another low groan, the wall split, and the two halves swung up from the middle, exposing a deep black cavern below.

A stench worse than that of rotting garbage escaped from the darkness and smacked Javi in the face, making him stagger backward. He pinched his nose to keep from gagging.

As he stared in disbelief, the shimmering shadow lifted Nico into the air and floated him into the cavern. Before the little boy disappeared, a gust of wind snatched off his red cap and whisked it into the woods.

Then the wooden doors creaked and groaned and swung back into place with a *thud* so permanent, so final, it brought Javi's heart to his throat. The tree trunk rolled back over the doors, sealing the cavern as tightly as a crypt.

"NICO!"

Javi collapsed onto the wooden doors, pounding and crying and yelling his brother's name. He put his ear to the door and listened. He could hear only the wind howling around him and the rain beating on the wooden planks.

Javi sat back on his heels. He examined the doors. They were old and heavy and the hinges were rusty, but he could probably open them if it weren't for the huge log pinning them down.

Think—don't panic, he told himself. *Think!*

He pushed his whole weight against the heavy trunk. It wouldn't budge.

He surveyed the clearing, looking for a strong stick or branch, anything he could use as leverage. The doors were tilted downward, and with some leverage, he might be able to push the log enough to start it rolling.

At the edge of the woods he found what he needed—a thick branch about his height. He half dragged, half carried it to the cavern doors.

Standing atop the wooden doors, facing the downhill tilt, Javi jammed one end of the branch against the log. He held the other end against his shoulder and pushed. He put all his weight into it, but the log still wouldn't budge.

What was he doing wrong?

He remembered how his father had told him that a person could lift several times his own weight with just a good strong stick to use as leverage. He'd even shown him how. But now something was wrong.

Javi pushed until his shoulder was sore. Still nothing.

Then it came to him. He was pushing the branch against the log, not using it as leverage.

Javi heaved up the branch and wedged it under the log so it stood up by itself at an angle. When he was satisfied the branch was solid, he grabbed the free end with both hands and lifted his feet off the ground, hanging from the branch with all his weight. The log groaned and came loose.

The next moment, Javi was lying face up on the doors, with the branch on his belly. The tree trunk had rolled off the doors.

He scrambled to his feet. Under the spot where the log had been lying, he found two rusty iron rings. He made the sign of the cross, said a quick prayer, and tugged on one of the rings. As he had suspected, the doors were heavy, but he was able to pull up one, then the other, until the cavern was in full view.

The odor that drifted out was foul, but not as nasty as when the doors had first opened. The cavern was dank and musty and pitch-black. Javi shone his flashlight down the hole. A rickety ladder led about ten feet down to a dirt floor. The walls appeared to be lined with stone.

"Nico?" Javi whispered. "Nico, can you hear me?" He poked his head inside the hole. "Nico?" he said a bit louder.

He thought he heard something. He leaned in farther. Was that a whimper?

He shone his light toward the sound. Nico, crouched in the corner, stared up wide-eyed. His dirty, tear-streaked face twisted and his mouth opened in a silent scream.

"Don't be afraid, Nico. It's me, Javi. Everything's going to be all right, you'll see. Just step to the ladder. Hurry, Nico. Come to the ladder. I'll help you up."

Nico cowered, taking terrified peeks at the wall across from him. He crouched farther into the corner and buried his face in his knees. He shook his head.

"Nico," Javi tried again, "don't be afraid. I've come to take you home. Just stand up and come to the ladder. Hurry!"

Nico shook his head again and whimpered.

Javi gave a frustrated sigh. "Okay, Nico, I'm coming down. Don't worry, I'll have you out in a few minutes, then we can go home."

Javi switched off his flashlight and clipped it to his belt. Saying another quick prayer, he stepped onto the first rung and began his descent. At the third rung he felt a hard tug on the back of his slicker and heard a sharp *crack!*

His foot broke through the rotted rung, and a force pulled him backward off the ladder.

As Javi fell, time seemed to slow. He was aware of his arms and legs flailing as he tried to grab something to break his fall. He heard Nico scream his name. He felt his body hit the dirt, knocking the wind out of him and bouncing his head. He heard the bone in his leg break as it twisted under him. And as the explosion of pain and colors filled his brain, he saw the wooden doors swing up and close overhead.

Then he sank into blessed darkness.

"Javi! Javi!"

Someone was shaking him. Javi groaned. His head throbbed. Hot pain radiated up his left leg and into his back. The shaking continued. It made the pain worse.

"Stop," he moaned. "Stop shaking me."

"Javi, you're awake." It was Nico. His voice trembled.

Javi opened his eyes. Even that tiny motion hurt. He moved his eyes but could see only darkness.

"Javi, are you okay?" Nico whined. "Please talk to me."

"Where—where are we? Why are the lights out?"

"We're in a cave. In the woods, I think. Javi, I'm scared. I thought you got killed. I thought you left me like Mami and Papi did."

Javi blinked, trying to adjust his eyes to the darkness. He strained to see. "I won't leave you, Nico," he managed to say. "I'll never leave you. Just help me remember. Tell me what happened."

"The evil one," Nico whispered in his ear. "He chased me and Hamish. He brought me in here. Then you came. But the evil one pulled you down. He hurt you. He wants to keep us here . . . with Hamish."

As Nico spoke, bits of memory returned to Javi, fleeting images. Nico in his yellow slicker running over the bridge, dropping Pulito; Javi running through the woods, then using his psychic abilities to track his brother; the clearing, the doors in the ground, the stench, the shimmering shadow, his fall off the ladder . . .

"Hamish," Javi muttered, "you were chasing Hamish. Then Hamish brought you here."

"This is where the evil one is keeping him prisoner."

"And now he has us?" Javi's heart lurched as reality hit. He had to get out of there. He had to get them *both* out of there. Javi tried to sit up. *"Aaa-yiii!"* The pain was incredible.

"Javi, you are hurt?" Nico placed a cold hand on Javi's face.

"I think . . . my leg is broken. I can't move it. Nico, get the flashlight. I clipped it to my belt."

Nico's hands felt along Javi's chest and down to his waist. When he reached the flashlight, he fumbled with the clip until it was free. A tunnel of light snapped on.

"Move the light around, Nico. Let me see what this place looks like."

Nico obeyed. The light showed rough stone walls dripping with moisture. They formed a small, rectangular room about the size of his bedroom. It appeared to be a cellar or shelter of some sort. A rotting ladder led up to the double wooden doors in the ceiling. The third rung of the ladder was broken.

Javi winced, remembering his fall.

The area behind the ladder was cluttered with boxes. Next to the boxes sat a tiny cot. At its foot lay a bundle of blankets.

"Nico, shine the light on the cot and hold it steady."

There also appeared to be a small bundle on the bed and maybe some clothes, but from Javi's vantage point, it was hard to tell.

"Nico, can you see what's on the bed?"

Nico let out a tiny whimper.

"What's wrong? What do you see?"

"I don't want to look. That's where the evil one waits."

"The evil one? Is he here right now?"

"No. He left after you fell."

"Is Hamish here?"

"Hamish is afraid. Hamish is hiding."

Great, Javi thought. *Now he's hiding. Why couldn't he have stayed in hiding forever and left Nico alone?*

"Listen, Nico, turn off the flashlight."

"Nooo," Nico whined. "I'm afraid."

"We have to conserve the battery. The battery won't last forever, and we'll need it later. Don't worry, I'm with you. Here, take Pulito, he's on my belt. That's it. Okay, now sit right here, next to me, and hold Pulito. Good. Turn off the light."

Nico snapped off the light. Javi closed his eyes and tried to concentrate. He pushed his hands against the hard dirt floor, feeling for psychic energy.

Through the blackness came the sounds of sobbing, constant, inconsolable sobbing. Javi felt Nico scoot in closer. But the sobs were not coming from the little boy next to him; they seemed to emanate from the corner where the little cot sat. The sobs grew louder, almost deafening, filling the darkness, filling his mind.

Javi's chest shuddered with uncontrollable spasms. The sobs were inside him, pulling at his heart, at his gut. He could barely breathe for the spasms that shook his lungs.

Then a bone-snapping coldness enveloped him.

A faint glow caught his attention. He turned his head toward the cot. A small boy was kneeling on the tiny bed.

Next to the bed, a lantern illuminated the scene. The boy's blond curls bounced as his body shook with sobs, the same sobs that were consuming Javi.

"Mama, Papa," the boy wailed, "please come take me home. I want to go home."

The cellar doors creaked open, sucking icy wind and rain into the tiny shelter. A man bundled in a heavy coat and hat began to climb down the ladder. The ladder creaked, but the third rung was still intact.

The wind gave a ghostly wail as the doors thumped closed.

"Stop that whining, kid!" the man bellowed.

The sobbing stopped instantly, dissolving into tiny hiccups and occasional gulps.

"Here. I brought more food." The man pulled a burlap bag from his immense coat and tossed it onto the cot. "Even picked up some of them licorice bits you're always bellyaching about. Should keep you quiet for a while."

"I want to go home," the little boy muttered, ignoring the bag.

"Yeah, yeah, we all do. But first your pa has to pay up. If all goes well, we should both be outta here by tomorrow night."

"Papa is coming?" The boy sat up straight, his eyes full of hope.

"Yeah, that's right," the man said with a grunt. He pulled a sheet of paper from his coat and examined it under the light of the lantern. "Soon as I get this here letter to him telling him where to leave the money. Just gotta wait until dark, then I'll sneak up to the house and leave—"

His next words were drowned out by a crack of lightning, a roar of thunder, and the sickening sound of splitting wood. A deafening *creeeaak, CRASH!* rattled the cellar doors and shook the ladder. Dirt and dust rained down from the ceiling.

The boy screamed and jumped onto the cot, shrinking into the wall.

The man spun around and looked up. The sheet of paper slipped from his fingers and floated to the ground. "What the—?"

The rest was lost in a coughing fit brought on by falling dirt and dust particles in the air. The man yanked off his hat and flapped it about, trying to clear the air. He ran to the ladder and scrambled up the rungs.

He pushed, he banged, he shoved his body against the doors. But they would not give. With a string of profanities, he began banging against the doors again.

"C'mon, you stupid pieces of—*ahhh!*" More dirt and particles rained on his head. He covered his face and rubbed his eyes. After a few minutes he resumed banging and yelling. "What the hell is going on?"

"Mister?" said a tiny voice. "Mister, what's wrong?"

"Shut up, kid. I don't need it from you right now!"

The man continued to hammer with his fists and bang the doors with his head. Then he stepped up one rung, until his shoulders were touching the doors, and he heaved. His body trembled from the strain, and he grunted like a large animal in intense pain. After a few minutes of rest, he began again, heaving and grunting, heaving and grunting.

"Damn lightning must've brought down that rotten tree," he muttered between grunts.

"Mister, please . . . I'm frightened."

Ignoring the boy, the man stepped off the ladder and dug behind the boxes. He pulled out a long, heavy stick.

Climbing halfway up the ladder, he wedged the stick at the edge of the doors and pulled. Wood creaked; the man puffed. With the crack of a rifle, the stick snapped in half, and the man fell to the ground yelling more profanities. He grabbed the two halves of the stick and flung them into a corner. He climbed back up the ladder, inspecting the situation.

"Mister, please—"

The man scrambled down the ladder and ran to the cot. "I told you to shut up!" The man hollered so loud, veins stuck out at his throat. "Looks like we're trapped in here, and if we are, I don't want to spend my last hours with a kid whining in my ears. So shut up, or I'll make you shut up!"

Returning to the top of the ladder, the man shoved his shoulders against the doors and heaved. He continued the process, heaving and resting, until he suddenly stopped and cried out in pain. He stumbled down the ladder and doubled over, clutching his left arm.

The boy ventured to the edge of the cot. "Mister, what is it?" he whispered.

"Pain, down my arm, ripping my chest. *Ahhh!* Too much pain." He staggered toward the boy, but fell to the floor at the foot of the cot. He curled up, still clutching his left arm. "Help me . . . help . . ."

The little boy slipped off the cot and went to the man's side. "How can I help, Mister? What can I do?"

"Don't know . . . trapped . . . cold . . ."

While the man tossed back and forth and groaned in pain, the boy went to one of the boxes and pulled out two blankets. He covered the man. Then he knelt beside him and waited. When the man ceased to move, the boy shook him.

"Mister, wake up, please wake up. I'm frightened, Mister. Please wake up. Tell me what to do."

Finally the boy stood and crawled back onto his cot. The sobs started again.

As the sobs began to consume his body, Javi opened his eyes and pulled his mind away from the scene. It was too sad, too terrible to think about. That poor little boy. Poor little Hamish. What a horrid fate.

But if Javi didn't get them out of there, it would also be their fate . . . his and Nico's.

"NICO," SAID JAVI, struggling to sit up, "turn on the flashlight. Then give it to me."

When Nico handed him the flashlight, he pointed it toward the cot. Nico turned away. The bundle at the foot of the cot was in the same place the man had fallen. The bundle looked like blankets covering something. On the cot where Hamish had lain, there appeared to be another blanket-covered mound.

Dios mio, Javi thought. *It's them. We have to get out of here. And in the meantime I can't let Nico know what's in that corner.*

"Nico," he said, "you have to help me move. I've got to get us out of here, but I can't do it alone."

"I can help, Javi. I will help you." Nico bent down and tried to pull his brother up by the shoulders.

"*Aaa-yiii*— No, Nico, that won't work. It just hurts more. Help me make a splint. Maybe if we stabilize the broken bones, it won't hurt as much."

"What do I do?"

Javi shone the light around, trying to find pieces of wood. "There, in that corner. See those two sticks? Grab those and bring them here."

Javi recognized them as the two halves of the long stick that had broken when the kidnapper had tried to leverage the doors open. They were about thigh high on him—a bit long, but they would have to do.

"Now I need something to bind them up." Javi shone the light around again. He thought of the boxes next to the cot, but he couldn't ask Nico to go near there.

"Will my scarf work?" Nico opened his slicker and produced a blue woolen scarf.

Javi stared at the scarf in wonder. "Oh, Nico, you were wearing your scarf?"

"It's so cold here in California. And it was raining . . ."

"Of course, that's wonderful!"

Javi slid his Swiss Army knife from his pants pocket. Because the knife had been his father's, it was well equipped. He pulled out the tiny scissors and cut the scarf into long strips. While Nico held the pieces of wood to either side of his leg, Javi slowly wrapped the strips around the splints, as he'd seen done in the movies.

Each time he moved, knife-sharp pains shot up his leg and into his spine. The pain paralyzed his lungs so he could barely breathe. Javi bit his teeth together to keep from screaming. Drops of sweat ran down his face. His hands shook. He had to stop a few times to regain his courage, but finally the splints were secure.

After Javi rested for a few minutes, Nico helped him drag himself to the ladder. Even the slightest movement hurt, but Javi squeezed his eyes against the shooting pains and tried to focus on getting them out of there. By hanging on to the rungs, Javi was able to lift himself to a standing position.

"Javi, you can't go up there. The ladder is broken."

"I have to. It's our only chance. I'll be careful this time."

"What if . . . what if the evil one . . ."

"Nico, forget the evil one. He can't keep us in here forever. I won't let him. Now, step away so you won't get hurt if I stumble. And hold the light on me so I can see."

When Nico had stepped against the wall, Javi began to climb. His entire body trembled with pain. He could put no weight on his injured leg, so he pulled with his arms and slid his good leg up to the next rung. Fortunately his arms were still well muscled from years of swimming. He climbed slowly, glancing around periodically to see if the evil ghost would try to stop him.

At the fourth rung he was able to push against the doors with his hands. But as hard as he pushed, the doors refused to budge. Realization of what had happened hit him in the stomach: The evil one had rolled the dead tree back over the doors.

No wonder the ghost allowed him to climb the ladder. He and Nico were trapped—just as Hamish and the evil one had been.

A deathly cold descended on Javi. He felt as if he'd been dunked in an icy pond in the dead of winter. It was the same cold he had felt when the evil one had enveloped Nico. The ladder shook and a strange vibration filled the air. Laughter. Wild, hysterical, horrible laughter. It rattled the doors, vibrated his eardrums, and made bitter nausea tug at the back of his throat.

"Javi!" Nico wailed. "I'm scared, Javi!"

"Nico! Don't listen to him—listen to me! Come here, hurry!"

Nico ran to the ladder.

"Climb up the ladder, in front of me, facing me. Hurry!"

Nico quickly obeyed.

"Now clip the flashlight onto my belt. That's it. Place your hands through the rungs, like this, and hold on to me. Don't let go no matter what happens, okay? Don't let go!"

Javi put both his hands on the doors above him.

"You can't have us, you hear me?" he yelled at the evil one. "You can't keep us here!"

The horrid laughter continued.

His pain forgotten, Javi glanced around, expecting to see the shimmering shadow of the evil spirit hovering nearby. He saw nothing. His skin crawled, trying to slink away. His intestines turned to gelatin and sloshed inside him. The disembodied laughter was more terrifying than if accompanied by the apparition of its phantom owner.

Javi closed his eyes, trying to set aside his terror, and concentrated. He locked onto the laughter, the cruelty of a man who could kidnap a small child and keep him trapped for days in this miserable dungeon, the waste of a young, precious life, the grief of the boy's parents. All this wickedness, and from the grave, the kidnapper's spirit laughed. He had them trapped as he had been trapped, and now he laughed.

Anger rose in Javi, strong and fierce. It bubbled in his stomach, it raced through his veins, it pumped in his heart. This cruel, wicked thing would not take his brother! It would not take him! If ensuring their freedom took the last ounce of energy he had, he would make sure that the evil one would not gain two more victims. With that thought, Javi pushed up, up, up against the doors, both with his arms and with his mind.

"Mami, Papi, help me!" he cried.

A groan, a creak, and a loud, rolling rumble made him push harder. "Hold on, Nico, hold on!" Suddenly the doors burst free, and his lungs filled with fresh, cool air. The wind was still blowing, but the rain had stopped.

"Get up, Nico," Javi told him. "Get up and out—hurry!"

He helped the little boy pull himself up the ladder and flop onto the wet grass above. At that moment a chilling scream pierced Javi's eardrums. The scream was one of rage and hatred and scorn. It paralyzed Javi's limbs, muddled his brain. In that second of hesitation, Javi felt a strong yank at the back of his slicker.

He was thrown off balance, and his good foot nearly slipped off the rung, but a tiny hand caught the neck of his shirt and held him in place. Nico's grasp was surprisingly strong. He clung to Javi and pulled. In response, Javi gripped the ladder with all his strength and hoisted himself up. All the while, Nico pulled and tugged, helping his brother to safety.

When they were both above ground, Nico helped Javi close the cellar doors.

Javi heaved himself onto the doors but could go no farther. "I can't walk, Nico. I'd send you ahead, but I can't let you get lost in the woods. We can't stay here, either. Who knows if that wicked thing will try again? If only I'd been able to find Tití's cell phone."

"I have it." Holding Pulito in one arm, Nico pulled the cell phone from the pocket of his slicker.

"The phone! You had this all along? And you didn't tell me?"

"You didn't ask. And I forgot."

"No wonder I couldn't find it." Shaking his head in disbelief, Javi grabbed the tiny phone and dialed his aunt's number.

He listened, but there was no dial tone. He tried again. Still nothing. He shook the phone and dialed once more.

Javi groaned. "The battery's dead. Now wha—"

Above the whining wind, he thought he heard his name. He listened.

"Javi! Nicolás!"

Javi's head snapped toward the sound. His gaze scanned the woods, but he saw no one.

"Nico, did you hear—?"

"Javi! Nicolás!" The voices seemed to be getting closer.

"It's Tití!" Before Javi could stop him, Nico darted toward the woods, screaming, "Tití! Tití, we're here! We're here!"

"No, Nico, come back! You might get lost." As Javi struggled to his feet, his aunt, followed by two men, emerged through the trees. In the next moment, Nico had flown to her side and was scooped up in her arms.

Above them, a circling crow called, "Caw, caw, caw!" and then flew off.

"LOOK, JAVI," WILLO WHISPERED, pointing to the woods in the backyard.

Javi looked where she indicated. On the footbridge stood a doe, as still as the trees around her. Only her ears moved, sifting out sounds of possible danger. Her eyes, dark as onyx, observed them with detached interest. Behind her a small fawn stepped away from a bush and joined her.

Willo stifled a squeal of delight. "Oh, have you ever seen anything so beautiful?"

Javi shook his head, too full of emotion to answer.

In the next instant, mother and fawn darted into the brush and were gone. A blue jay shrieked overhead. A mockingbird replied with a mimicking cry. Two squirrels scampered down the trunk of the old oak and scrambled across the bridge.

"It's so peaceful here, now that the evil thing is gone," Willo commented.

"Yes, I never saw so many animals on this side of the woods before," Javi replied. "It is as if they know it is safe now."

One month had passed since Javi and Nico had been rescued. Javi rested his cast on the chair in front of him. It had been signed by everyone he knew in California: Willo signed first, then Amparo, Nico, Willo's dad, his orthopedist, his psychologist, and all the members of the reading group, even Ms. Watkins and Robert. In another month the cast would come off, and he'd start swimming again. But he intended to keep the cast as a trophy of his ordeal.

"So there's been no more sign of the ghosts?" Willo asked.

"Not since the day Tití and your father found us outside that old cellar."

Willo made a face. "Daddy said it was horrible. He went inside the cellar after the paramedics took you and Nico to the hospital. I hadn't wanted to tell you before, but he said the bodies were almost mummified. Probably from being sealed in that cellar for so long."

Javi shivered despite the warm sunshine. "I have been wondering why that cellar is out there in the woods."

"The cops told Daddy it was probably an old root cellar that belonged to a house that was destroyed or torn down years before little Hamish was kidnapped. No one remembered it was out there. That's why they never found the bodies—until you stumbled on it."

"I am glad they were able to find proof that the bodies were of Hamish and his kidnapper without my help. I did not want to have to explain that I knew who they were because I had seen their ghosts. The kidnapper's letter was still on the ground where he dropped it, and it was still readable."

"Legible," Willo corrected. "It's nice that Hamish's relatives still live in the area and were able to have him buried next to his parents. That's probably what the little guy wanted all along—to be found and taken back to his parents. Even if it had to be after he was dead."

"Taking the kidnapper's body away and burying it, even in an unmarked grave, probably helped his ghost rest, too."

Willo nodded. "Interesting that they never found out who he was."

"He was a very bad man," Javi said, remembering. "I am glad he is gone."

"It seems all the bad things are gone—even your poltergeist. No more occurrences of recurrent, spontaneous psychokinesis?"

"No, but I was fortunate to have had psychic abilities while Nico was lost."

"No kidding. I couldn't believe you actually rolled away that dead tree and opened the cellar doors with your mind. You never told Amparo, did you?"

"No. I believe my psychic abilities are gone now, anyway. They would be too difficult to explain if I could not prove them. I would rather forget all of that."

"I can understand." Changing the subject, Willo asked, "How has Nico been?"

"Nico doesn't even mention Hamish anymore. He cried at first because he missed him. But since Tití enrolled him in TumbleGym, all he can talk about is Zoe and Sam. Now Tití tries to make sure that Zoe and Sam come over as often as possible."

Willo turned to Javi and regarded him with cool gray-green eyes. "You're both very lucky to have Amparo, you know."

A ghost of a smile crossed Javi's lips. "I know."

After Willo left, Javi heard a strange sound toward the front of the house. The hair on the back of his neck prickled. The old feeling of dread returned. He stepped into the hallway and listened. The sound of sobs and sniffles mingled with giggles drifted from the family room.

He poked his head in the door. Amparo sat on the floor with her back to him. Two shipping boxes lay at her side, and items from the boxes were spread on the floor in front of her.

"Tití?" he said, stepping next to her.

Amparo looked up. Her face was tear streaked, and her nose was red. But her face shone with happiness.

"Tití, what happened?"

Amparo held out her arms to him. He went to her, and she held him tight. Then she gave an embarrassed little laugh and pulled away.

"Nothing is wrong, *mi amor*. Your old aunt is being *boba*. Silly and maudlin and nostalgic."

Javi knelt beside her on one leg, extending his plastered leg before him. "Why? What is all this?"

"It's a care package from your Tití Luisa. A delightful care package full of all sorts of wondrous things. Look, just wait till Nico gets home from TumbleGym. We'll have a feast."

Javi eased his cast into a comfortable position and sat beside her on the floor. He began sifting through the treasures. "Homemade coconut candy?"

"Yes, Luisa made it. And look, she collected most of

your mami's recipes from friends and neighbors and from your *abuelita,* and she wrote them all down on these cards. You know how your mami always kept everything in her head. She never even wrote down her recipes. But she shared them, so Luisa was able to re-create all of your favorites.

"And look at this box—it's full of food: *bacalao*—salted codfish, and *carne vieja*—remember the aged, salted beef? And she made fresh *pasteles,* wrapped in real banana leaves, and your favorite—*lechón asado.*"

"She sent roast pig and *pasteles?* How?"

"She packed everything in plastic bags of ice and sent it by overnight mail. But there's more, look! Fresh white cheese and guava paste, and this—Puerto Rican candy— sesame bars, and lollipops—*pirulí*! Here, have one." Amparo unwrapped a cone-shaped, multicolored lollipop for each of them and promptly stuck one in her cheek, swirling it around like a little kid. "I can't believe she did all this! It reminded me so much of when I was a girl in Puerto Rico that I started crying. Silly, huh?"

Javi glanced at his aunt. He shook his head, remembering what these things meant to him. "No, not so silly." It made him feel good to know they had that in common.

"And look at this." Amparo held up a cassette tape. "It's a tape of *coquí* voices."

"*Coquí* voices?" Javi laughed and took the tape, checking out the photo of a tiny tan tree frog sitting on a leaf three times its size. "What's it for?"

"So you can listen to it sometimes and be reminded of nights back home. You could even listen to it when you go to bed, to help you sleep. I told Luisa how much you missed the song of the tree frogs at night, and she must have remembered."

Javi grinned. "That was nice of her."

"Yes, it was. And there's one more big surprise." Amparo's eyes regarded him fondly.

"What?" Javi glanced around, looking for the surprise.

"It's not here, it's back home."

Javi's heart jumped. Was she sending them back to Puerto Rico? Two months ago, that would have been the best news in the world, besides finding out that it had all been a mistake and his parents were really alive and well. But now he didn't really care where he lived, so long as the two people he loved most were there with him.

A chill as cold as the evil one's breath consumed him. Was he going to lose Amparo now, after all they'd gone through?

"Hey"—Amparo laughed—"don't look so gloomy. I said it was good news, remember? You look like I told you Ms. Watkins is going to live with us for a week."

Javi forced a smile. He had to pretend that whatever happened, he didn't care.

"Boy, that's a big improvement. Now you look like you swallowed a chili pepper whole."

Javi grinned.

"That's much better. Okay, here's the thing. When you and Nico came to live with us, the family had to figure out what to do with your parents' house."

"Mami and Papi's house?"

"Yes, you see, there was still a mortgage to be paid on it, and we didn't know what their finances were like." Amparo paused and looked at Javi. "Oh, don't look like that. I keep telling you it's good news. Everything's fine. Your parents left you boys well provided for. But we didn't know at first, so we had planned to sell the house—"

"Sell Mami and Papi's house?"

"Well, yes. You couldn't live there alone, and the mortgage would have had to be paid. Usually the only thing to do in these cases is to sell off the property, pay the mortgage, and put the rest in trust for the kids."

"Oh." It made sense, but Javi hadn't really thought of other people living in his old home. It made him feel as though he'd lost something else that was dear to him. If selling his old house was the good news, what was the bad?

"But as it turns out, your parents both had plenty of life insurance to provide for you kids, and your papi's retirement account is substantial. You and Nico will have plenty to attend any colleges of your choice and be well provided for after that. In the meantime, you're my responsibility, so I'll provide for you."

"What does all that mean?"

"It means that all the money your parents left, except maybe a small monthly allowance for you and Nico, will be invested and kept in a trust fund until you're in college. And we won't have to sell your old house. Luisita and your uncle will rent it out until you're twenty-one. Then if you want to move back to Puerto Rico and live in it you can. Or you and Nico can sell it. It's yours—both of yours."

"I . . . I can go back to our old house to live someday?"

"Mm-hmm." Amparo nodded with a happy smile. "And, of course, you can go back and visit your cousins and old friends on vacations."

Javi felt a rush of relief. A heavy weight rolled away, like the dead tree rolling off the cellar's doors. "But in the meantime Nico and I stay here . . . with you?"

"Well, of course, you stay here. Where else would you go?" Then she paused. "Is there somewhere you'd rather be?"

A grin that came from deep in his heart spread across Javi's face. "No, there's nowhere I'd rather be."

"Co-KEE! Co-KEE!" sang a tree frog. "Co-KEE! Co-KEE!" answered another.

Javi smiled as his room filled with the cheery night song of the tiny tree frogs. After a dinner of roast pig and stuffed banana leaves, Javi had taken some candy and a few other items from Luisa's care package up to his room, where he popped the *coquí* tape in his stereo.

He placed the candy in his candy drawer and pinned a miniature souvenir *pava*—the traditional Puerto Rican straw hat worn by country folk—to his bulletin board. Luisa had also sent him a ceramic green leaf with a tiny brown tree frog squatting in the middle. He placed the ceramic *coquí*-on-a-leaf on his nightstand next to the framed photos of his family.

His parents smiled happily at him from an eight-by-ten, and next to it, the four of them, Nico, Javi, Mami, and Papi, grinned in front of Sleeping Beauty's palace at Disney World. He scooted the two frames apart and placed his newest framed photo between them. It was the one of Nico and himself standing on either side of Amparo, who was wearing a tall white chef's hat and grinning from ear to ear. Behind them a plump chicken roasted on the rotisserie of the indoor barbecue. At their feet, and doggie-grinning into the camera, sat Fidel; beside him ZsaZsa and Misifú glared haughtily. This was Javi's family. His new family.

Javi snapped off the *coquí* tape and opened the window. The air was fresh, and the night was filled with the chirping of crickets. Once in a while, from the edge of the creek, a bullfrog croaked. The little creek, now back to its normal size, gurgled in harmony to the other night songs.

The *coquí* tape was nice, and it would be great to listen to the tree frogs when he felt homesick, but the crickets and the bullfrogs and the creek sang him to sleep now. He would sleep to the song of the *coquí* on his visits back to Puerto Rico.

Javi got ready for bed. As he lay in the dark, listening to the night sounds, he tried, just for the heck of it, to move things around with his mind. He stared at his digital clock and concentrated. Nothing. He stared at his computer chair, trying to make the seat spin around on its pole. Still nothing. He stared at the model airplanes that waited patiently on his shelves.

Nothing moved.

He sighed. Ah, well—*qué pena*. He would just have to get used to being a normal, eleven-year-old kid.

As his eyelids drooped from the weight of exhaustion, and his mind drifted to another place, the green numbers on his digital clock began to flash; numbers whizzed by at incredible speed. The seat of his computer chair spun on its pole, and his five model airplanes lifted off the shelves and zoomed around the room.

After a few moments the planes landed back on the shelves, the chair froze in place, and the digital numbers zipped back to normal time.